THE CHRISTMAS SONGBIRD

Emma Hardwick

COPYRIGHT

Title: The Christmas Songbird

First published in 2020

Copyright © 2020 Emma Hardwick

ISBN: 9798720394066 (Paperback)

BOOK CARD

Other books by Emma Hardwick

The Urchin of Walton Hall

Forging the Shilling Girl

The Sailor's Lost Daughters

The Scullery Maid's Salvation

The Widow of the Valley

The Slum Lady

The Vicar's Wife

The Lost Girl's Beacon of Hope

CONTENTS

PROLOGUE

From the first time that Suzanna Stratton looked down upon the stage at The Songbird, she watched the artists in awe. She knew, without a shadow of a doubt, she wanted to be a singer—and a famous singer at that.

But she wasn't in a posh, plush box when she felt the calling. The precocious eight-year-old had secretly climbed up into the theatre's rafters from the attic space she shared with her seamstress mother.

From her unique vantage point, the young girl could watch the performers, as well as the bustling activity behind the curtain. As chaotic as it was backstage, the presentation of the performances was flawless. Captivated by the entertainment on show, the audiences were unaware of just how many people it took to fill their evenings with such pleasure and delight.

Suzanna had not found the small niche by accident, but with David Liebowitz, the owner's son, during one of their many adventures exploring the nooks and crannies of the old music hall. He had held her tiny hand, and she had tagged along behind him in the darkness unnoticed. Reaching their hiding place had been quite an obstacle course. It began with shimmying into a crawl space. They would wriggle through the gap and tiptoe unnoticed towards a flight of steel stairs. Then he would pick up her tiny frame. Her trusting little arms clasped around his neck for all she was worth as he made a precarious light-footed jump over some missing floorboards and onto a narrow wooden promontory high above the stage. From there, the pair could look on undetected.

Once she knew how to get to the secret viewing point, Suzanna sneaked off to see as many performances as possible when her mother was at work.

David was five when Suzanna was born, and he was fascinated by the infant. He had no siblings, and as Suzanna became older, he took her under his wing. Everywhere that he went, she followed. He was the big brother she would never have, and she, his little sister.

If her mother had known that Suzanna was up in the rafters every night, she would have got the beating of her life, but Maria Stratton worked punishingly long hours as a seamstress. As soon as the curtain came down, Suzanna would sneak back to the attic, and by the time Maria got back from putting the costumes away, the little girl would be safe in her bed, pretending to be asleep.

Suzanna attended school in the morning. It was the only time that she felt she had to deal with reality. Other than that annoyance, she lived in a world of sublime fantasy.

The Stratton's flat in the attic wasn't a proper dwelling as such, but rather one of a series of large storage spaces tied to the theatre, filled with props, furniture and screens from shows gone by.

When Maria was at work, Suzanna was at peace to rearrange the furniture to her liking. In her mind, she had lived in Paris, Greece and many more exotic destinations. Suzanna would open boxes of costumes and spend her afternoons pretending to be queens, pirates, fairies or any other fantastical role that suited her mood. It was the burlesque outfits that she enjoyed the most because she loved the rapport the risqué singers built with the crowd. She had memorised every song in their repertoires. On many a long, lonely evening, she would perform the tunes with gusto on a makeshift stage built out of old wooden crates, dreaming of the chance she would get to perform for real.

Maria made very few demands of her daughter, besides going to school and being safe. She was a free spirit too, and she did not expect her daughter to live a bleak, working-class life. Maria craved the opportunity to give her all the freedom that she never had as a child. Watching her daughter's imagination develop and her confidence build was a joy for the beleaguered single mother.

The old theatre in Covent Garden was Susanna's oyster, and in her uninhibited child's mind, she was a pearl. The cheerful girl was much loved by the small community of like-minded people around her, a happy mixture of misfits who had become a true family.

1

THE TRAVELLERS COME TO TOWN

St. Giles in the east end of London was Maria Stratton's birthplace and its slums, a portal to hell itself. Every day was a bitter grind, with only the occasional moment of joy to punctuate the gloom.

"So, yer pregnant are yer, yer hussy," her father had yelled when she announced her predicament. "Where are yer and yer grubby little bairn goin' te live then? Not under my roof, I tell you. Find yersel' a hole to crawl into and don't ye come back 'ere. I am ashamed of yer, do you hear me! Ashamed."

He raised his hand to strike her then thought better of it. While the argument raged, Maria's mother swiftly packed her daughter's clothing into a bag. Furious, the father shoved the young girl through the front door and onto the dark cobbled street. The small bag of belongings sailed through the air and skidded by her feet.

"I never want to see ye again, lass. Ye made ye bed, now lie in it."

Neither parent were particular adherents to morals, but it was an excellent opportunity to get rid of their young and increasingly wayward daughter and save a few more pennies to put towards their liquid diet.

Alone in the narrow lane, with the spring rain showering down upon her, Maria put her hand on her belly, desperate to be close to the only family member she had left. The filthy tenement buildings looming overhead added to her feeling of anxiety, and she felt as if she was suffocating. She ran toward the bustling marketplace and sheltered under a shop's awning for a moment. The situation in the market was as dire as anywhere else in St. Giles, but at least it was a dry space where she could take a moment to catch her breath and focus on her predicament, and a few bystanders made her less at risk of being mugged for the few pennies she might have on her.

*

Maria knew who the father of her child was, but if she had disclosed it to her father, he would have been more than berserk—he would have throttled her. She had met the man in question near the Seven Dials district. Standing on a street corner playing the violin, he had a hat laying on the ground in front of his feet. The most mournful tune Maria had ever heard, for her raw emotion was communicated through each note of the arrangement.

She stopped to listen to the musician as he bared his soul in public—the only person in a stream of many who was able to comprehend the suffering behind the music. Ocean saw Maria observing him intently and looked into her eyes. At that moment, the spark hit her soul and her heart raced. She felt as though he was playing the music just for her. It was a peculiar encounter, but strangely enjoyable. Exciting, even.

A few days later she bumped into the violinist again, this time at St. Giles market when he was at work—not as a musician this time. Now, his trade appeared to be far less glamourous, a humble builder's labourer. Instantly remembering the beautiful young woman who had watched him play, he doffed his flat cap and winked at her. Maria smiled coyly from across the street. Interpreting the smile as a good sign, Ocean put down his hammer and walked towards her.

"Good day, Miss. Forgive me, but I saw you
listening to my music last week."

Maria felt shy. She had not realised that she had been so obvious, and she hoped nobody else had seen her fawning over the fellow. *If word gets back to Pa, I'll be for the high jump.*

"Don't worry," he said, smiling reassuringly as
if reading her worried thoughts. "Most people

don't understand my music. It's like I am invisible to them. It washes over them, and they go along doing their usual business. You caught my attention because you stopped to listen."

"It was such a sad tune," Maria sighed.

"My people have experienced a lot of sadness. I am impressed that you sensed that. It is a traditional Roma song—an Eastern European sound of suffering."

Ocean smiled at her. The dark-skinned man was exotic looking. She did not know what to make of him. There were so many stories and warnings about Gypsies, so she kept at arm's length, being cautious not to seem over-familiar.

"Where did you learn to play the violin?" Maria asked.

"My father taught me. He loved music."

"It is very different from our English tunes."

"Of course it is. We play with our soul."

"What does that mean?" Maria quizzed.

"It's not only a pretty little ditty. Our music makes you feel emotions—joy, sorrow and passion."

Maria blushed. The men she knew never discussed these matters of the heart so openly. She began to regret asking. Ocean noted her embarrassment.

"Please don't worry about enjoying my music, Miss. Thank you for the compliment."

"My name is Maria," she exclaimed nervously, not wanting the encounter to end, even though she felt her inexperienced face reddening.

"Well, Miss Maria, it has been a pleasure, but now I need to go back to work before my brother finds me loafing."

As he walked away, he stopped and looked over his shoulder.

"Forgive my rudeness. I'm Ocean. Ocean Taylor. Perhaps, I'll see you again, Maria?"

With that, she watched him disappear into the crowded market. Ocean Taylor seemed so intense, not like any the other pimps and drunkards she had met in St. Giles. *And what a name!*

"Ocean," she murmured to herself dreamily.

The young eighteen-year-old dawdled home, her head filled with thoughts of the soulful swarthy young man. Itching to tell someone about him, she stopped in at her friend's house on the way home.

"Bernie, I met a chap called Ocean today," Maria said hesitantly.

"Oh yeah? That's an odd name," Bernie replied.

"Yes, it is, He's a Gypsy."

"Oh, Maria, if yer wants peace in yer life, it's best you stay away from a Gypsy. Yer father'll skin you alive."

"But—he was so nice, Bernie. There's something quite special about him," she added with a cheeky glint in her eye.

"Let it go, Maria, it will only cause trouble. They only marry their own," Bernie advised her as her eyebrows raised ever higher. "I can't see yer waltzing around England in a bleedin' Romany caravan telling fortunes."

Maria started to laugh.

"You're right, neither can I," Maria agreed with a chuckle, "but don't discount it just yet, I am sure it would pay better than my sewing job with Mrs Turner."

Following Bernie's advice, Maria put all thoughts of Ocean Taylor aside as she navigated her way through the dirty streets to the small flat the Strattons called home.

Her mother had made a slop of sorts. The woman was too lazy to cook properly. Her signature dish was boiling whatever they had in the house to a mush and disguising whatever flavour was left with oodles of salt and pepper. Maria's useless lump of a father sat drunk in front of the fire.

The girl gulped down a bowl of the bland grey goo then escaped up the stairs to the family bedroom, hoping for a few precious moments of privacy before the end of the day and the inevitable crush of bodies on their lone mattress.

*

Every winter the Gypsies set up camp in the area at Seven Dials, and they offered their usual services as tinkers, handymen, musicians and fortune-tellers. In addition to their legitimate skills, they also had the reputation for being pickpockets and small-time thieves. There were plenty of rumours of them stealing children too. Most of the permanent residents were so woeful at caring for their families they often lost tabs on their offspring's whereabouts. It was far easier to accuse the travellers than admit that they were poor parents who neglected their children.

The local criminals liked to use the Gypsy visit as a cover for their nefarious exploits, revelling in blaming their crimes on the influx of travellers. Still, for the bulk of the locals, the Gypsies had their novel appeal. They dressed differently and had their own language. Although they looked poor, they adorned themselves with masses of gold and silver jewellery. What's more, they brought lively entertainment: laughter, music, and the most beautiful women dancing free and unashamedly in the firelight.

It was a cold December night when Maria Stratton left work late on the fateful Saturday night of Suzanna's probable conception. Miss Kelly was snowed under with orders for alterations to dresses for the festive season and demanded all her girls did lots of overtime. All Maria seemed to do was work, work, work. The long days were exhausting but the extra money was helpful.

Maria followed her regular route home through Seven Dials. The evening was cold, but there was no rain. As she passed the Gypsy camp, she saw that a big crowd had gathered around the warmth of their bonfire. Curious to see what was happening, she passed along the periphery of the great crowd, craning her neck as she peeped through the gaps between the sea of heads and shoulders.

In the centre, she saw the raging red flames reaching up to the night sky and the community of Gypsy women dancing around it. The women seemed carefree and joyous, uninhibited and free of the rigorous Victorian social demands that the English women had to endure. Maria felt envious. The romance and freedom appealed to her.

Her thoughts were interrupted by a voice behind her.

"Good evening, Miss."

She looked around, startled. There was Ocean Taylor, smiling broadly and his dark eyes sparkling in the firelight. He oozed a free-spirited charm and carnal experience that Maria found intoxicating.

"Come with me!" he whispered seductively in her ear as he grabbed her hand.

"I can't! I mustn't!" she protested meekly.

He gave her no option as he gently pulled her into a narrow alley. She gave him a nervous smile, delighted that he had taken the lead. It was like a dream come true, a chance to escape the dreariness of the slums. Once hidden from sight, he kissed her, but it was not the usual fumbling experience she had from time to time with the boys who fancied her in her childhood—this was pure, manly fire.

For the first time in her young life, a man had awoken her passion. As she experienced the delights of desire, Maria suppressed her moral urge to stop him. Ocean was keen to take things as far as he could.

"I want more," he murmured, his mouth close to her ear once again.

She could feel his hot breath and rough stubble brush against her soft face. His swarthy rough hand lifted her dress and touched her smooth thigh. There was no attempt to stop him. She revelled in the reckless freedom. It was exhilaration and liberation that she had never known before. This was the life she wanted, a life free of the heavy responsibility of tomorrow.

He hustled her into a nearby Roma caravan, lifted her up like a fairy-tale princess and softly lay her onto a bunk. She watched him hop up alongside her. He pulled the curtain around them with a brisk swish and began to remove his clothes. She had never seen a man this close naked before, and she was torn between her head saying she should be bashful and look away and her heart urging her to stare at his muscular physique.

Deftly, he teased each piece of clothing off her until she too lay naked and expectantly before him. Ocean made love to her passionately, and she responded in the same way. She had heard that the first time for a woman was painful and unsatisfying, but that was not what she was experiencing. It was exquisite. There was no talk of love. There were no promises of a future together. There were no invitations to ride off with him into the sunset. It was pure lust and it was fabulous.

When Ocean's family returned to the van for the night, Maria gently pushed her lover away, her eyes wide with panic. Ocean seemed relaxed about it. He propped himself up on his elbow and put his finger against his grinning lips. His family seemed to be worse for wear from drinking and all the fireside partying and quickly tumbled into their beds. The young couple hid behind the curtain in silence and quietly continued their carnal exploration of each other's bodies when they were sure the others were asleep. Alas, Maria started to imagine her parents back at home worrying about where she'd got to. The dark thoughts began to overtake her feelings of joy, and with regret, she said it was time for them to call it a night.

Ocean walked her home and then kissed her goodnight in the dark shadows where nobody could see. It had been the best night of her eighteen years, and she wanted to live it again, every single moment. A feeling of pure excitement tugged at her heart as she closed the front door. She waved at him through the grimy front window and watched him slip away.

Upstairs, she could hear her mother and father were snoring drunkenly. She crawled into their bed and fell asleep instantly.

In the morning, Maria's mother and father interrogated her about where she was the night before, but the only reply they could get out of her was 'with friends down the boozer.'

On Sunday evening, she casually strolled to the Gypsy camp and made her way toward Ocean's family van. His mother was sitting in front of it, cooking something on an open fire, and she greeted Maria in a friendly manner.

"Ocean," she yelled loudly.

He emerged from the van drowsily.

"Oh, Maria," he said with a smile, "come in."

This time she pulled him onto the bunk and shut the curtain.

*

Maria was so cheerful on Monday morning, even her parents commented on her mood.

"Did ye have another good night out with yer mates then, lass?" her mother asked.

"Yes, Ma! Loved every second of it!"

"Well look at 'em rosy cheeks and that smile! Perhaps, you should get out more often. That Miss Kelly works you too hard. Our girl's gotta have some fun, eh, Archie?"

"I hope it's not a man, yer little trollop," grizzled her father spitefully, sensing she was not being straight with them.

Maria was not very fond of her parents, and she muttered a few curses under her breath as she washed the breakfast dishes. Archibald Stratton was a filthy unemployable slacker, and her mother Doris was a fat, foul-mouthed fish wife. If nothing else the last two nights had taught her that she wanted freedom and that she would never be satisfied with an ordinary life.

The morning was freezing. With the belching chimneys and dark clouds overhead, it was pitch dark as she left for work. Still, despite the gloom, the streets were busy. Maria made her way through the alleys merging with the grey mass of foot traffic with their heads bent and shoulders hunched, wending their way to their places of work. Age was irrelevant. Amongst the old and frail, there were children as young as eight shuffling along, barely awake, off to eke out a meagre living.

As she reached the market square, the traders were erecting their stalls, fighting against the dim light. Fires next to their trestles kept them warm but left a cloud of thick smoke hovered over the square. Maria felt there was something a little different about the site this morning. It seemed emptier. She walked down the street, pushed her way through the bustle of the market, and then realised what was missing—the Gypsy camp.

2

SEAMSTRESS
REQUIRED

Two months later Maria realised that she was pregnant. She did not launch into hysterics, and she did not care what people thought, she simply cast her mind back to the two nights in the caravan and decided that it was worth the whole experience and that she would make sure that the child would bring her great joy. *Anything that can break my mundane day to day life is welcome.* The most fantastic favour her parents could have bestowed upon her was to evict her. When they did, she was relieved and prepared. She took her little bag and headed to see her childhood friend, Bernice.

"I need a place to sleep for a short while. Can you help me, Bernie?"

"Me ma and da should be alright wiv it if you give them a few bob a week. I'll ask them."

The matter was settled. Maria moved in with Bernie and her family. They were all a bit taken aback one evening when Maria informed them in a very matter-of-fact tone that she was pregnant.

"Oh, dear God, lass! Who is the father?" enquired Mrs Ridley.

"Don't worry, Ma'. He's long gone." Bernie exclaimed as she came to Maria's aid. "But his name will be on the birth certificate. And she'll be able to work for ages yet."

"Come and speak to us if you need help, Maria. We can't make no promises, but we will do our best."

How different these people were to her own family. Maria knew that it was a disgrace to have a child out of wedlock, but something in that fateful night with Ocean had set her free.

She made a solemn promise to herself. Nobody would ever victimise her or her child and that she would live her life on her terms. St. Giles was chock full of alcoholics, paedophiles, incest and murder. A baby out of wedlock was hardly a crime in comparison. It did not even make the top ten list of sins that Reverend Whitfield preached warnings about in church every Sunday. God help those who tried to torment her—she would have nothing of it.

*

Her employer, Miss Kelly, did not take the news well. It was getting harder to disguise the bump with her clothes, so Maria decided it was best to confess to her predicament. As a virtuous spinster of sixty, she was horrified to hear that Maria was with child.

"Oh my!" she exclaimed. "What will people think? You'll be the talk of the town!"

Maria shrugged her shoulders, unsure of what to say to the woman.

"My dear, have you told your parents yet? They must be devastated."

"Yes. They were upset," Maria replied.

"Have you been to see the priest, gone to confession?"

Maria was not a Catholic, so she remained silent.

"Well, my dear, you have to understand that even though I am very fond of you, and you are an excellent seamstress, it will cause a scandal if I retain your services. If our more religious clients find out, I may as well close my doors."

Maria nodded her resignation. She had no option but to respect Miss Kelly's wishes.

"That said, I am sure you could use the extra money so I am happy for you to stay for a week or two more until your bump shows too much, then, regretfully, you must leave. Will you do me a favour, petal, and wear your big overcoat on your walk into work?"

Even this small reprieve for Maria filled Miss Kelly with anxiety. The following morning the old lady went to the local Catholic Church and said her confession. Then she lit candles and donated money to the poor box in an effort to alleviate her all-consuming guilt.

Maria continued working for another month. She would be lying if she said she had no concern about the future, but she did not feel hopeless. There had to be a solution. Her instincts told her she would never end up in the workhouse. Far too resourceful and resilient to give in, she was determined to take any opportunity that came her way, hoping the future would bring something more exciting than a one-roomed home for her and the child in the slums of St. Giles.

On her last day at work, Miss Kelly and the girls surprised Maria with a leaving do. They had collected some money and gave her a beautiful quilt that they had made for the baby. Their kindness filled Maria with emotion, and she realised that despite Miss Kelly's strict adherence to religious and social norms, she was a forgiving soul.

"When all the dust blows over, and the bairn is a good size, I will gladly have you back, petal," Miss Kelly reassured Maria.

The expectant mother felt a lump in her throat and her eyes watered.

> "Thank you for everything you have done for me. I will always remember it."

The girls wished her luck and from behind the grimy windows waved her goodbye. Most of them lived in St. Giles they hoped Maria would probably bump into them, but still hurt as much as if she were leaving for good. In a reflective mood, she returned to her friend's house.

*

> "The girls collected enough money for me so that I can stay here for a month."

> "Aw lass, it's not like me ma will put yer on the street, like," Bernie answered.

> "Yeah, I know Bernie, but they have bills too. Can't expect them to keep me."

> "It's going to be hard to find a job being as round as you are," laughed Bernie.

> " I have this feeling that something big is about to happen."

> "Yeah, that big thing growing in your belly is about to happen!"

Maria chuckled, then her smile turned to a frown.

"No, Bernie," Maria sighed, "a new life—a new start."

Bernie watched her friend struggle up the stairs, clutching the quilt. She felt for her. *It's a terrible predicament. Rather her than me.*

Maria's desperation to leave the claustrophobic little house grew day by day. The weather had turned foul, and she could not go out for a week. Finally, there was a break in the storm clouds. She dressed up warmly, took her umbrella and set out on a walk through the market.

Her stomach had grown in a surprisingly large in a very short while. There was no mistaking her pregnancy. Locals lifted their eyebrows when they saw her and whispered behind their hands. Others greeted her as usual and pretended that they did not notice. If Maria had been a sensitive type, she would have dropped her head in shame and hurried through the lanes, but she was not. Maria had an unusual personality. She lacked a pronounced rebellious streak, yet she did not care what anybody thought of her. *Worrying about other people's opinions of me solves nothing. Might as well get on with life.*

*

Maria decided to take a stroll toward Covent Garden, a place she enjoyed immensely but seldom had time to visit. She turned into a lane just off Seven Dials and walked down a cobbled street, lined with inviting tea and coffee shops, pubs and a few eateries. A few crossings further on, she saw a sizeable building standing proudly in the row. The frontage was decidedly ornate. It could have been an old school or perhaps a church. It had large imposing doors decorated with carvings. Elaborate wrought-iron lights adorned the steps. Above the door was a sign:

'THE SONGBIRD THEATRE'

It was then the penny dropped about the posters lining the neighbouring walls advertising acts and shows. There were pictures of beautiful ladies in risqué costumes, comedians in garish chequered suits, singers with their arms outstretched holding a note perfectly and all sorts of exotic wonders and novelty acts the like of which she had never seen before. Maria was fascinated.

Next to the building ran a long thin alleyway which lead to an open space. A small sign on the wall read 'Deliveries'. Out of sheer curiosity, Maria walked down the path and reached some tall buildings surrounding a vast courtyard. There was a heavy wooden stage door at the top of a small flight of steps. The sound of a beer barrel being rolled along by one of the staff startled her. Feeling like a trespasser, she trotted back to the road before she was discovered. She turned back to see if she had escaped unseen. It was then another sign caught her eye:

'SEAMSTRESSES WANTED
APPLY WITHIN'

This is the chance I've felt in my bones for days now. Boldly, she returned to the stage door, knocked confidently, cranked the stiff handle down and walked in. A cheerful, rosy-cheeked woman of about sixty opened the door.

"Who are you looking for lass?"

She did not take notice of Maria's protruding stomach.

"Well, I saw the seamstress job advertised—" Maria explained with a smile.

"—hold on, let me find Max the owner," the woman advised.

Before she left, the kindly woman gave her tired but happy-looking guest a cup of tea and sat her down at the large kitchen table, a table so large that Maria thought it could seat at least thirty people. She began to wait for what seemed like an eternity. Politely pacing herself with the tea it had gone stone cold, but she still sipped at it to look like she had a reason to be there. Her anxiety increased the longer she waited. She hid her nerves by smiling politely at whoever walked through the kitchen, just in case it was the owner turning up unannounced.

Twenty minutes later, Max Liebowitz appeared. He was an energetic fortyish man, with a cheeky smile and cheerful demeanour. He had a strong European accent that Maria could not quite identify. She struggled to understand what he was saying at times. Thankfully, she picked up on an important question amongst his jabbering.

"Do you have experience as a seamstress?" he enquired hopefully.

"Yes, Sir. Miss Kelly down on Mandrake Street employed me for three years."

Maria felt his gaze sink and settle on her round stomach.

"We are snowed under with work, so the hours are long. Will that be a problem?"

"No, Sir. I am a very hard worker. Miss Kelly will tell you that."

"And, err—" Max paused as he took a deep breath. "When is your baby due?"

"Not for a while yet. Months," she replied earnestly.

Mr Leibowitz didn't give any clue as to his thoughts on the pregnancy. Maria dreaded continuing the conversation, but as Bernie often reminded her: 'beggars can't be choosers,' she feigned confidence.

"I will need accommodation, as well. Perhaps you have a room for us. Even a bit of a storeroom floor would do where we can lay a mattress. A roof over my head is all I ask for. My family have disowned me because of the bairn, and I am too proud for the workhouse. I have been relying on the generosity of friends.

I will work hard, I promise. All I ask is that you give me a chance to prove my worth to you."

"I tell you what. I'll give you a room in the loft if you're prepared to put in the late nights," Max bargained.

Maria smiled from ear to ear.

"I can assure you late nights are not a problem. Thank you."

"It's a pleasure," he confirmed, grinning from ear to ear. "We're a somewhat messy and chaotic family here at The Songbird, but we are a happy bunch."

"When do I start?" Maria enquired.

"Immediately," said Max. "Go and fetch your things from that friend of yours. I'll get my assistant Thomas to clear a space for you. We'll have you settled in no time."

That was twenty-one years ago, and Maria had never looked back at her dull life in St. Giles. She had never gone back to see her parents, and she never tried to find Ocean again.

3

THE SONGBIRD THEATRE

Max Liebowitz stood proudly, hidden in the wings, as he looked out into the auditorium. For decades, he had stood on the same spot watching the patrons arrive. He watched their delight and anticipation as the curtain was rising. He saw smiles develop on people's faces as they were spirited away into a fantasy world of music, wonder, illusion and laughter. Providing them with a welcome escape from the grim reality of life outside the theatre gave him a tremendous sense of purpose and a feeling of pure joy.

Thomas Bartlett looked at the older man and smiled with affection. He had accompanied Max to the stage every night for the last five years, and every night Max said the same thing:

"Ah, look at that, Thomas. Just look at that crowd—see how they are enjoying

themselves! That is what life is about,"
announced Liebowitz in his Polish accent,
which had softened over the years. "Life
should be full of laughter, and we make them
laugh, Thomas."

Max Liebowitz was the most unreasonable person to work with that twenty-eight-year-old Thomas Bartlett had ever met. Nevertheless, he adored the cantankerous old fellow. Over the years, Mr Liebowitz had become like a father to him. Max was a born dreamer, and Thomas was the aide who was always tasked to make those dreams come true, however far-fetched or awkward they might be. Max cherished Thomas' level-headed support.

After being roundly defeated by his employer's errant and excitable behaviour, Thomas had given up trying to clip Max's wings. As soon as Thomas surrendered and did as he was asked, without question, he realised that Max's unusual philosophy on life was inspirational, joyous and uplifting—even if his frequent splurges on fun and frivolity for the audience were eye-wateringly expensive.

"How do you always remain so cheerful, Max?
No matter how challenging life is or the
challenges we face putting on the shows, you
always remain joyful?"

"Ah Thomas, there is so much misery in the
world. I bought The Songbird because I
wanted to see people smile. The greatest

lesson I learnt is that you can't make other people happy if you aren't happy yourself. It is a great privilege being responsible for the happiness of others, whether it be your family, friends or beyond. When the audience and our little backstage family are happy, so am I."

Max's son David was a little less tolerant of his father's well-intentioned but wayward nature when it came to the theatre's finances.

"Papa, this place is chaos," David would lecture him. "The performers take advantage of you. You have families housed in the attic who do not pay for food or rent, and there is a constant demand upon you to support the local charities," he complained.

Max, however, would just smoke his cigar and laugh, which frustrated David all the more. The young accountant felt his father needed to appreciate some home truths.

"You never count the takings at the end of the night. I have concrete proof the doorman steals. The bar has never balanced since I've worked here—and you're continually allowing the poor entry without paying," he chastised.

"We are blessed, David. There is enough for everybody. I live a better life than all the people in Covent Garden. I have a small house

to call my own, a bed, food on my table every
night and loyal employees who are happy to
work with me. What more does a man need?"

Thomas would sigh when he heard David trying to
reason with his father.

"He's right, Max."

"Don't you worry about anything, my boy.
Leave the finances to David," Max would
remind Thomas.

Thomas would shake his head. For him, Max the
dreamer and his son David the realist were worlds
apart. Any hope of being the bridge between their
contrasting viewpoints and getting the theatre on a
solid financial footing seemed to be doomed.

"David told me that he is looking for another
job. He says that this is not a theatre, but a
circus, run by a clown."

"My son David has been telling me that for
years," Max chuckled. "My boy is a very
shrewd businessman. His business acumen
has kept The Songbird alive for many years—
on paper. I have kept it alive in people's
hearts."

"David is right about a lot of things, and if we
didn't have him here, we would have closed
the doors years ago. You mustn't push him
over the edge and force him to leave to save

his sanity. We need him here." Thomas said firmly.

Max nodded yet again as his aid's advice washed over him unheeded.

"I love my son, yet I wish that he would stop worrying about me."

"I'm sure he cherishes you too, Max. You raised him alone without a mother to care for him. He's turned into a fine man."

Max smiled fondly at the mention of his beloved wife.

"David needs to marry and have children! He is nearly thirty years old with no problems in life—and that is why he has time to worry about the small things in mine."

Thomas listened with a smile as Max chatted about his son.

"He is so busy that he has no marriage prospects. It concerns me. I want grandchildren."

"You have the whole neighbourhood's children here most of the time—for free, I might add. You treat them all as if they were your own. I think you need to take David's business advice occasionally. He is a trained accountant."

"And then I would have no fun! Stop complaining, for goodness' sake, Thomas," Max whined playfully. "And you? Are you fretting or happy here?" the old man asked with a wry smile.

"Of course I am happy. I will never be this content anywhere else," Thomas reassured.

"Quite right too, my lad. What else does a man need besides happiness and enough money to look after a family? That is success my boy, not the lavish but empty life that the elite display for all to admire."

Thomas liked the sound of what Max was saying, felt the old man had rose-tinted glasses on about The Songbird's future.

"Max, some of the performers use you at every opportunity that they get. They are paid the best wages in the city, but they constantly demand more. What is worse, you indulge them," he lamented.

"Thomas, my good man, talented performers are the foundation of our business. They draw a full house to our theatre every night. Of course, they have an ego, but our patrons would never return to The Songbird again and again if we did not have loyal performers. I can't see why rewarding them for their contribution is such a difficult idea for you to grasp."

"Max, you are such a stubborn man," Thomas moaned.

Max deflected the focus of the conversation back onto his assistant.

"When are you getting married, Thomas? Go and find a nice girl and start a family. You and David do not understand the joy that children bring. You are getting older as we speak. A wife is essential to a man's happiness."

"Well, that is a fine comment coming from you, Max? What happened to you wife? In all these years, you never talk about her."

"Ah, Thomas, " sighed Max as he became more serious, "that is a long story for another day."

At times like this in their conversations, Thomas knew that it was no use going any further. Max would squeeze his shoulder and walk away into the shadows of the colossal theatre, lost and distant.

Over the years, Thomas had learned how to make his own life easier: stop complaining. Instead of criticising Max's grand dreams and schemes, he put all his efforts into bringing them to fruition. Max, David and Thomas became inseparable, forming an unbreakable, if awkward, alliance.

Late at night, when the chaos of the day had subsided, Thomas would lay in bed wondering what happened to Max's wife. No matter how often he gently encouraged his boss to explain, no answers were forthcoming. *One day, he will tell me what happened to her.*

*

David Liebowitz was trying hard to keep his temper. The handsome man's desk was covered with a mound of administrative papers, and every time he looked up, one of his staff had put another invoice or letter on top. Most of the letters were addressed directly to Max. Some of the correspondence contained the most unreasonable of requests. David would try and dissuade his father from reading them in case he was tempted to help. Still, Max would usually open each letter and read it out loud. Then, he would insist upon replying to each one personally irrespective of whether he could assist or not. In desperation, recently David had demanded that Max appoint a secretary who could help him.

"Let me read that, David," he would demand of his son.

If David refused, Max would try and second guess the subject matter.

"It is the local orphanage asking for a Christmas donation? I bet it is. How much do they need?"

"It is indeed, Papa. They are having a special yuletide meal for the orphans at the workhouse. They are asking for a donation of twenty pounds."

"Send it to them, David. Those children deserve a full belly, especially in the festive season. Have you seen that wretched orphanage? Send them the money."

David would carefully observe his father in those moments. If he gave Max even the slightest hint of disapproval, his father would give him his usual response, perhaps to educate him or maybe even to spite him.

"We are all God's children, David. Give them the money."

David had given up lecturing his father on their financial woes. Instead, he had honed his creative skills and juggled the meagre finances in an attempt to keep everybody happy and the lights on.

"Trust me, David. That small gift will bring great happiness to those children. We are compelled to look after the widows and the orphans at our gates."

David had heard his father's words so often that he had conceded already and had put twenty pounds into an envelope and addressed it to the orphanage. In return, Max would receive another lovely letter of thanks, and David would place it in the bottom drawer of his desk, with all the others.

Drowning in paperwork and late invoice payment requests, David could no longer keep up with Max's correspondence. The task was so gigantic that he spent four tedious months trying to find a suitable secretary for his father. None of the clerks that David appointed were suitable for the post. Whether they were men or women, they never lasted very long. None of them could cope with Max's eccentricities. Ultimately, Max's patience with the recruitment process petered out.

"This is useless, David. Can't you just find someone who knows the business? Someone in this building? Someone that I like? And someone who likes me?" Max demanded.

David rolled his eyes. The problem was not if Max liked them or not, but rather whether the new employee could tolerate Max's endless challenges.

It was Thomas who solved the problem. For the umpteenth time, David had to accept another resignation from a clerk who could not endure Max. David thought that he had struck gold since the latest one had lasted the most extended period to date—a whole month, rather than a week. However, when Max decided to take a brief holiday, leaving the poor woman to take on all the responsibilities alone, she became so overwhelmed by the task at hand, that she preferred to resign rather than have a mental breakdown from the strain.

"What about young Suzanna, Maria Stratton's daughter?" Thomas posed.

"That is a jolly good idea!" David exclaimed in glee, before stopping in his tracks and muttering ominously, "But do you think Suzanna will want to do the work? I mean, she's working in the sewing room at the moment, and it's peaceful there. Max's administrative tasks are—not quite so peaceful."

"She'll be fine. She has gone to school, can read, write and do sums. Besides, Max has a soft spot for her, and it is reciprocated. Why not give her a chance? You and Suzanna have been friends for years and you'll make a good team. You won't have to try and gel with another new starter. The worst that can happen is that she resigns and goes back to the sewing room," Thomas mused with a chuckle.

David smiled at Thomas and wished that he had thought of it four months earlier. Suzanna would be the perfect person for the job.

*

As time went on, Suzanna wasn't sure that working for Max was such a blessing after all. As much as she loved his bubbly and enthusiastic demeanour, he was exhausting. No sooner had he engaged her in one task when his mind changed, and he demanded another. She was by no means overworked, just befuddled by all the chopping and changing. Thankfully, through hearing the mutterings of her colleagues, she was reasonably knowledgeable about what was happening at The Songbird and more often than not, she took the initiative in solving the inevitable problems caused by Max's erratic decision making.

Yet, Suzanna was harbouring a secret. Like her mother, she had a wilder side to her personality, crying out to be expressed. Just after she started as Max's assistant, she had seen a run-down pub advertising for a singer. There was nothing for it, she felt compelled to apply.

The owner, Tim, a brash Yorkshireman, listened to her sing a few ditties. He looked at her beautiful face, then let his gaze drift down to her ample bosom and curves. It was then he decided that she would be more than suitable for the position.

"Now me girl, yer might have the voice of an angel, but yer got to show a little flesh to my punters too. It's not as posh as The Songbird here. When you come back, bring a costume that shows your legs, and prop up that bust of yours a little more."

Suzanna nodded shyly. It was the first time a man had spoken to her in this manner.

"Our customers like a more daring show. Do you think you're up to it?"

"Of course," she replied with confidence,
despite having only seen burlesque shows,
rather than starring in one.

Her mind drifted off towards the necessary preparations. *A sly raid of the costume crates in the attic is bound to turn up something perfect to wear.* She had watched the shows at The Songbird so often and practised all the steps in her room. Suzanna was quite sure she was going to bring down the house when it was her time to shine.

"Oh, and what's yer name, petal?" Tim
enquired.

"Suzanna Stratton," she answered.

"No, lass. Yer stage name?"

"I, err, don't have one yet," she mumbled
apologetically.

"Well, let's call you Milly Martin."

It was not a name that Suzanna would have chosen, but it would do for now.

*

On Saturdays, Suzanna knew that Max only got to The Songbird after dark. *It will be easy to sneak out before he arrives.* Her smile widened as she filled a large bag with her costume, stage make-up, a mirror and a brush. The stage outfit that she had liked best had a tight-fitting bodice, and her imprisoned bosom had no choice but to flow voluptuously over the top of the stiffened material. *Tim will approve.* The bodice was attached to the skirt, which fluffed around her like a ballerina's tutu. She suspected that if she bent down, the audience might get the faintest glimpse of her frilly bloomers. *Perfect.* She wore sheer silk stockings on her long shapely legs. Dancing shoes with a heel completed the ensemble. The whole outfit in red and black looked striking and Suzanna deemed it bawdy enough to get everybody's attention. After a few nights secretly practising on her makeshift stage in the attic, reviewing her performance in a full-length mirror, she had the utmost confidence in her ability.

Finally, the night for her debut had arrived. David saw her as she sneaked out past his office, the big bag banging against her legs as she tiptoed out of the building. He was too busy with someone else to call out to her there and then. Luckily for him, a couple of minutes later, he was free. He grabbed his hat and his coat, hoping that he could catch up with Suzanna and take her for a drink, mainly to apologise for his father's latest vacillations. He couldn't bear the thought of having to find a replacement for Max just yet. *A bit of gratitude won't go amiss.*

The overly-eager Suzanna was well ahead of David but he could just still see her. He followed her down the street until she stopped in front of a boozer, The Crown and Cushion. He walked towards the pub with curiosity. He pushed open the double swing doors and looked about him, but she had vanished. David ordered a pint at the bar, his eyes darting around looking for clues to her whereabouts. He decided the owner had tried hard to make the place look grand, but his efforts had been a consummate failure. The place was shabby, and so were the Saturday night crowd who had gathered there. *Suzanna must have given me the slip? A dive like this isn't her sort of place, surely?*

His eye was taken by a bright poster on the wall that said there would be a show starting downstairs at nine o'clock. Since Suzanna seemed to be missing, he decided he might as well go and see what the show was about. He chuckled as he knocked back the last of his pint. *I bet if my father was here, he would say this act is perfect for The Songbird! Somehow, I doubt it will be!*

*

In the cramped room in the basement that Tim said was 'the dressing room', Suzanna propped the face mirror up on a rickety table and steadied it against the wall. She took out the makeup and laid it out in front of her. The liquids and powders worked like magic, and as she applied them step by step, gradually, she became unrecognisable. She only became nervous when she began to put on the costume. Knowing she would be seen in public in it was very different from prancing around in private. The bodice was so restrictive, her breasts seemed to bubble up under her chin. She wanted to cross her legs and pull the short skirt down as far as she could when she caught a glimpse of her bloomers in a full-length mirror. Stunned by her reflection, she ignored her inner voice berating her for her outfit's lack of modesty and her lack of experience.

Tim's taken a chance on you. Now, it's time to see it through.

With no warning, she heard Tim behind her push open the door of the shabby closet open. He leaned against the wall and watched her do the finishing touches to her makeup.

"Stand up. Let me get a look at you," he ordered.

Suzanna obeyed shyly and straightened her pose.

"Now, turn to face me."

Keen to impress, she put her weight on her tiptoes, then elegantly spun in her dancing shoes, her skirt swishing around her quite revealingly and her ample bosom bouncing.

"Oh, that won't do at all. Come here!"

Puzzled, she glided over to him. Suddenly, Tim grabbed roughly at the front straps of her bodice and pulled it down an inch.

"The fellas don't want to see a nun, luv."

He looked her up and down and continued his judgemental assessment.

"And get rid of the silk. They prefer bare legs."

"What?" scowled Suzanna, aghast. *If this is what it takes to be a pub singer, I am not sure I want to be one anymore!*

"You are performing for people with very little imagination. Take off those stockings if you want to get paid tonight. Hurry up. You have two minutes to go."

*

The basement was damp and mildewed. Thankfully, the room lights were off, and there was only one large light shining on the small stage. There were six tables at the foot of the stage, all crowded with rowdy drinkers, each with a pint on the go, and at least another full one to follow to save queuing later. Behind them was a raised foot-high platform with a wrought-iron waist-high railing. Men of every class leaned over it, eager to watch the act. David formed an opinion on the clientele. They were a lewd and lively bunch and not what he was accustomed to at more refined The Songbird.

Off to the right of the stage, a skinny looking man with a cigarette smouldering in his mouth began to play a honky-tonk piano, and a thin and stained canvas backdrop fluttered down as it unfurled from the ceiling to cover the drab brick wall. The heavily made-up girl who appeared on stage was stunning, and there were wolf whistles and applause. Everybody was drunk and lustful, and there was a lot of crude references to her body. David felt uncomfortable with their lack of manners, and had he not been hemmed in, he would have left. He looked at the young woman on the stage, her chest was exposed more than it needed to be, and her legs were bare. *No wonder the boisterous chaps in the front row are on the prowl.*

*

When Tim pushed Suzanna onto the stage, she was instantly blinded by the spotlight. Terror struck when the piano started to play, and she realised that she had missed her queue. Thankfully, the pianist was experienced, and he improvised, allowing her to begin the song as if nothing had happened.

All Suzanna wanted to do was cover herself up. Practising alone on the makeshift stage in the attic had not prepared her for this. The tipsy patrons of The Songbird enjoyed themselves, but they only became raucous when the fresh air hit them as they tottered home. These men were crude from the outset.

David only knew that it was Suzanna when the singing voice rang out with 'My boyfriend is sitting in the gallery.' *It can't be her can it?* Before she'd finished the first verse, the men started to boo her. *Crikey, it is!*

"We don't wanna hear that old stuff!" shouted someone.

"Show us yer arse, girl!" cried another.

The poor girl belted out the lyrics, trying to drown them out. The pianist thrashed at the keys. It was useless.

"Tim! Oi! Tim! We want our money back."

A beleaguered Suzanna attempted to tame the rabble by trying some deliberately sensuous moves, but they ridiculed her even more, cruelly pointing and laughing. David was horrified by the direction the performance was taking—on and off stage. He began to push his way through the congested basement, trying to reach the front.

"Yeah, mate, I want to go home n 'all," laughed
a docker, his tobacco-stained teeth glinting
behind his thin lips.

By the time David got in between the front tables, the men were on their feet jeering. Suzanna was still singing and dancing trying to save the show when somebody threw a glass at the stage. Mercifully, she dodged it and it went crashing against the wall behind her. Two other hooligans did the same, and it was a miracle that none of the projectiles hit the poor girl.

One of the men grabbed David as he pushed past him.

"Where you think you're going, mate?" the
fellow shouted drunkenly.

David shrugged him off.

"You're after the hussy, ain'tcha?"

By now, David had enough. He turned around and punched the man in his mouth. The drunk lost his footing and he fell backwards into the crowd. People began to topple over like dominoes. It only took one punch, and the whole group started to brawl. Suzanna stood on the stage, a timid, terrified creature. She saw a man jump onto the small stage and her instincts told her to run—now.

David caught up with her and grabbed her arm.

"No," she cried out before she recognised him. "David!"

"I need to fetch my bag," she shouted.

"Leave it. We'll get crushed by that mob, run!"

David pushed her up the stairs, a little rougher than he would have liked, but now was not the time for polite indecisiveness. She turned back to look to him for reassurance.

"Go! Now!" he bellowed giving her another shove.

Tim, the landlord, was standing at the top of the steps, furious. The racket from the brawl was clearly audible above the noise in the main bar.

"You are going nowhere, Missy," Tim growled at Suzanna. "Someone's going to have to pay for the damage to my boozer!"

David sidestepped past Suzanna and grabbed Tim by the throat then stared into his eyes threateningly.

"She is coming with me, and she doesn't owe you any money. You're lucky I don't speak to the plod."

He pushed Tim aside, grabbed Suzanna's hand and pulled her out of the dive of a pub. The heavy swing doors flapped closed behind them. Even though it was quiet enough to talk now, neither one of them wanted to. The night was icy, and Suzanna's skimpy outfit meant she was barely dressed. David made her put on his heavy overcoat as they ran all the way back to the safety of The Songbird. They took one of the old service routes into the building to avoid attracting attention at the stage door. An apoplectic David dragged Suzanna to the attic and shoved her into her tiny room.

"What the hell were you thinking?" he roared at her.

Suzanna was too distraught to explain. She began to cry, and her makeup dribbled embarrassingly down her face.

"They would have killed you or worse."

The girl was sobbing her heart out as David paced up and down the room in silence for a few minutes.

"Come here," he said eventually, hoping a show of empathy might calm her down, but he was wrong. "Please, Suzanna, stop crying. What's done is done. At least you are safe now. And we got back without drawing attention to ourselves. It can be our secret. Just promise me you won't have another go at entertaining the rabble in a dockers' pub!"

Reassured that David was at least speaking to her again, she nodded then rubbed her face in an attempt to clean it, but ended up making the smears worse.

"Look at the state of you! Let me fetch a cloth."

David looked around for a flannel and some water as she stood in his large coat, looking like an orphan.

"Come here. Let's get you cleaned."

He took the rough and scratchy cloth and began to wipe her face until he had removed all the thick powder and paste. Then he cupped her face in his hands and laughed. Lightly. he prodded the tip of her nose with his forefinger and winked.

"You're much nicer without all that stuff on your mug."

Suzanna laughed weakly. She looked a complete quivering wreck. David put his brotherly arms around her and hugged her tightly.

"We will find a better way to make you famous," he whispered as he smoothed her matted and tear-soaked hair off her face.

Suzanna nodded, mortified by how her first night as a singer had turned out.

"Thank you," she said, sniffing loudly, as she handed back his coat.

"Now, get out of that horrid costume. Get a good night's sleep and we will laugh about it in the morning."

"Promise me you'll keep this matter to yourself, David? I couldn't bear the shame of it."

"You have my word. It is our secret."

"Max kept saying he would book me for a Saturday night, but nothing came of it. You know how he flits from one idea to another all the time."

David gave an exasperated sigh and a nod.

"All too well."

"I got impatient and I took the first opportunity that came my way. I've been such a fool. Now, I've made things worse. If he does offer me a slot on the bill here, I don't see how I can relax, David. Not after tonight's ordeal. The pub was supposed to be a way to get some experience and build my confidence. Now, I am terrified at the mere thought of appearing before a live audience again."

"Let's talk about it tomorrow when you are feeling better, shall we? Tonight is not a good time."

"Alright. Thank you for being there for me."

David kissed Suzanna on the forehead and bade her goodnight. He closed the door softly behind him and tiptoed downstairs. *What a night!*

*

In the morning, Suzanna's shame was unabated, and she did her best to avoid David all day. She had never suffered as much embarrassment as she did on stage at The Crown and Cushion. She felt violated by the incident and ashamed that the man she looked upon as a brother had seen her half-naked trying to titillate a room full of vile men.

By lunchtime, David knew he would have to break the ice with her. He ordered lunch for them from the kitchen and rescued her from Max's office and his never-ending list of errands.

"Come and eat with me. Cook's put our lunch in my office already."

Susanna froze.

"Hurry up, or it will get cold."

David tucked into his roast chicken and potatoes while Suzanna pushed her food around the plate.

"Do you want to be a singer?" he asked bluntly.

"Yes, and I wanted to do it without riding on Max's coattails."

"I admire that," David announced.

"You do?"

"Of course, it shows your character."

"Really?"

"Of course. You were brave enough to take a chance. It's just a pity you chose to start in a place where nobody could appreciate your singing voice."

"Do you think so?"

"I'm convinced of it. Tim knew those men wanted more than a song from you. You placed your trust in the wrong man. You know you can trust my father. He has a heart of gold. I'll speak to him. The best thing you can do is get on the stage here on Saturday night and sing your heart out. Show people your talent and what you're made of. If you don't do it now, you never will."

"What if someone recognises me from the Crown?"

"Trust me, Suzanna, I hardly recognised you in your Milly Martin stage outfit and we've known each other for years. I only knew it was you when you began to sing. Get out there and do it or you will always be sorry."

"I'll think about it. Please excuse me, but I don't have much of an appetite today."

She pushed the plate away from her then got up to leave. David watched her hips gently sway as she glided out of his office. She was stunning. After seeing a lot more of her flesh as Milly Martin, he realised she was a woman now—not the little girl who used to shadow him all over the theatre.

4

THE FRENCH DIVA

Mademoiselle Monique de la Marre, The Songbird's irascible diva, stood in front of the gilt-edged mirror admiring herself. Her blonde hair was perfectly coiffured into the latest sophisticated French style, and her midnight blue sequined dress was simple but tailored enough to display her sensuous curves. Her large blue eyes were the same colour as the dress, and her pale skin was flawless.

She was surrounded by so many women indulging her pre-show demands that the room looked like the boudoir of Marie Antoinette at Versailles.

"This needs to be parfait, oui?" she instructed her hairdresser, jabbing at the offending tress of hair that had tumbled out of place.

"I am not happy with this corset, Maria! How many times must I tell you that I am one size smaller? And the dress does not do my figure any justice," the prima donna hissed.

"Dear God!" Maria would explode when she was safely back in the sewing room. "Does she want her bloomin' bosom popping out during the show? Her thruppennies are barely contained by that bodice as it is. They are like caged animals fighting to escape. Mind you—it would be a good laugh if they did, wouldn't it? It'd bring her ladyship down a peg or two."

The seamstresses would burst out laughing as they imagined the furore such a display would cause. Every journalist in the city would be publishing it in the social columns the next morning.

Once Monique was satisfied her entourage had fussed around her sufficiently as she preened herself lovingly in the mirror, the shouting would recommence.

"Out! All of you, out! Allez! Vite!" Monique would yell in her French accent. "I need to be alone."

Everybody would scatter, relieved that they did not have to tolerate the ill-mannered woman any longer. Left alone, Monique dabbed her face with some powder for the umpteenth time and took a step back to admire herself in the mirror once more. In her mind, at last, she looked perfect. The moment was spoiled as her door creaked open.

Young Lord Peter Ashwood walked up behind her, putting his arms around her waist. He looked over her shoulder and studied her in the mirror, stroking his fiancée's bare arm tenderly.

"You are the most beautiful woman that I have ever known."

Perfunctorily, Monique smiled at him. So many men had said that to her that it made no impact anymore.

"I remember the first night that I saw you," he purred in her ear, doing his best to sound seductive.

"It was at a party, and I thought that you were the most magnificent creature. I sent you one hundred red roses the next morning, but I had no response from you. It all became clear when I visited you, and I realised that you had a room full of flowers from admirers already."

Monique ignored Lord Ashwood's loving words. Suddenly, he felt himself almost jumping out of his skin.

"Madeleine!" the diva shrieked at full volume. "Come in here at once! Where are you, you wretched girl?"

The sound of some sprinting footsteps skipped up the stairs, and the door swung wide open to reveal the breathless girl awaiting her latest set of instructions.

"I have to be on the stage in ten minutes. Find my diamond necklace and hurry up, oui? I expect Max has it in the safe," Monique ordered her maid. "Then go and see Maria and make sure the lining on my fur coat is repaired. Lord Ashwood and I are going to dinner after tonight's show."

Monique never—ever—said please or thank you. It was as if the words burnt her mouth.

"Yes, Mademoiselle," answered the harassed but attentive Madeleine, who quickly found the necklace on the dressing table already in front of her mistress.

Lord Ashwood looked on, stunned at the news that his fiancée would be dining with him, finally. She had rejected all his numerous advances of late, preferring to schmooze into the wee hours with her star-struck admirers.

"At the interval, tell Max there must be more bottles of chilled champagne in my dressing room that I can share with my visitors," demanded the shrew. "I want crystal glasses. Oh, and tell him to make sure that it is the vintage Dom Perignon, not that awful plonk Max seems to think is acceptable."

"Yes, Mademoiselle."

"And get the place tidy. It looks like a pigsty. I cannot entertain in this mess, d'accord?"

The young maid nodded, while the smitten Peter Ashwood stood in the background, watching Monique in adoration, accepting her rudeness as a case of Gallic nerves before her performance. He looked at the room around him. It was more of a salon than a dressing room. It was decorated in the palest pink and lilac, and the French furnishings were delicate. A large velvet chaise was strategically placed in the corner, allowing Monique to drape her curvaceous body over it while she held court. There was already expensive champagne on ice and a tray full of flutes stacked on a gilt table. Every available surface was covered with bouquets of blooms with sycophantic messages from her fans.

Peter Ashwood considered himself a lucky man to have met the young French beauty. Not only was she the most talented singer in London, but she came from a wealthy aristocratic family, with ties to the Austrian monarchy. What more could he wish for? She was not only beautiful, but she was rich as well. For the first time in his dull thirty-one years, thanks to his new sweetheart, the often-overlooked Peter Ashwood was now the talk of London's social set. He went to great lengths to ensure that the couple attended every public function that they could, a difficult task with someone as headstrong as Monique.

When he escorted the chanteuse to the stage, he heard the compliments and sighs of everybody who observed her. Peter knew that if she were to finally agree to a wedding date, he must become accustomed to all the attention she reciprocated to her admirers. He need not have worried too much, however, Monique believed that anyone Max employed or admitted to his theatre was a peasant and she was just going through the motions.

The French starlet stepped onto the stage, and the red velvet curtains swung open, their gilt-edged fringing lightly brushing the floor. The grand auditorium thundered with applause. The audience had come to The Songbird to listen to her angelic voice. She stood illuminated by the stage lights and started to sing, curiously feeding off the adoration of an English audience that she held way beneath her.

Suzanna stood in the wings, taking in Monique's flawless performance. She had spent months studying the confident young French woman. Although they were the same age, Suzanna thought Monique seemed so much older and more sophisticated.

As a lowly theatre assistant and a keen amateur singer with no formal training, Suzanna had been terrified to perform in front of Monique. It was only when her singing tutor, Mr Hoffman the theatre's conductor, threatened to cancel her practise sessions if she continued to shy away from performing that she had a change of heart. Firmly, he advised her that there would be no more training since other—more confident performers—needed his tutelage and she was wasting his time. Never would he have considered mentoring Suzanna if it were not for Monique openly criticising the girl's ambitions, and that Max seemed to dote on her like a daughter.

The compère took to his feet and began to announce the next act of the night, the comedian Champagne Charlie.

*

David stood in the wings at the other side of the stage, watching Suzanna prepare to perform. They had been friends since she learned to walk. Until now, David had always thought of her as a little sister, but imperceptibly for him, his feelings were slowly changing. For her, he was the big brother that she worshipped since childhood. As a youngster, the lad allowed her to follow him closer than his own shadow, never losing his patience, answering her endless barrage of questions about the theatre.

"You are performing tonight, oui?" Monique
whispered to Suzanna as she drifted
backstage towards her dressing room.

Suzanna nodded silently, not in the mood for a confrontation with the diva before singing in front of an audience for the first time since her disastrous appearance at the pub. Monique looked the nervous girl up and down, critically appraising her appearance.

"Why did you choose that plain white dress to
wear for your debut?" she asked
disparagingly.

Suzanna ignored her.

"It is so very—dull!" the egotistical singer prodded again, annoyed that she was getting no response out of the girl.

"I disagree," said Peter Ashwood, smiling at the dark beauty. "You look lovely, Suzanna."

For a second, Monique's temper flared, and she had to fight hard to contain her jealousy.

"Oh, Peter," she laughed. "You are such a kind man. How lovely it is that you try to make Suzanna feel better about herself."

Lord Ashwood frowned, not sure if the comment was a compliment meant for him, or a barbed insult directed at Suzanna.

Wondering what Monique was up to, David made his way over. He was perfectly groomed and looked striking in his immaculate black dinner suit.

"Well, David, you look handsome tonight! Are you going out with friends after the show?"

"Thank you, Monique. I am hoping to have dinner with a beautiful singer tonight. I have a table booked at The Ritz."

Monique giggled.

"Oh, that is so sweet of you. Unfortunately, Lord Ashcroft and I have plans for the

evening," said Monique presumptuously. "Do
you mind if David comes with us, Peter?"

David smiled charmingly before putting the poisonous
woman in her place.

"Oh, there's no need. I am sorry for the mix-
up, Monique. I was talking about Suzanna."

Suzanna heard the exchange and smiled. David was his
overprotective self as usual. One rare thing Suzanna did
agree with was Monique's assessment that he was
looking dashing that night. As she studied David, she
realised that she was jealous of the attention Monique
was wallowing upon him. Having never felt that way
before, it took Susanna by surprise.

Monique glared at David for the snub. He had humiliated
her time and time again in the past. Like all attractive
men she encountered, she had desired to seduce him
from the first moment that they met. Despite unleashing
a full charm offensive, David had never given her any
attention. His distancing forced her to be satisfied with
the likes of the pleasant dullard, Ashwood.

Max Liebowitz had infuriated Monique when he
informed her that Suzanna was to feature regularly in
the variety show. The French starlet did her best to
persuade him he was mistaken.

"You are such a sweet man, Max, but why are
you giving the girl false hope?" cooed a
patronising Monique. "You have the best show

in London, and now you want to spoil it because you feel sentimental towards a young woman, just because she has lived like a stray cat in your attic since she was a child?"

Max frowned at her protestations. In his mind, Suzanna had talent, and he felt no need to explain himself to Monique. The celebrity chanteuse might be a big draw for the audience, but backstage, she was exhausting with her constant petulance.

"Max, mon cher, the girl has been your secretary, and now she wants to be your singer as well. Perhaps, one day, she will become your spouse, oui?"

The remark infuriated Max, but he did not react to it. Everyone knew responding always added fuel to Monique's abrasive fire.

"She is the same age as you are, Monique. You and I have discussed this before. The girl has talent. She can sing. And with hard work—she may become as famous as you are."

"Sacré bleu, Max," drawled Monique. "It is not good enough to be talented. She has to dazzle her audience. I have trained at the Paris Opera under the tutelage of the finest maestros in Europe. Little Suzanna is reaching too high too soon, Max. She is bound to humiliate herself. She will be devastated, and you will be the laughing stock of London."

Max sighed and broke his golden rule of ignoring Monique's spiteful and selfish comments.

"Perhaps you can to teach her how to dazzle them, then?" he said, knowing full well that she would refuse, which would also annoy her. "Perhaps you can mentor her, Monique. You have nothing to fear, after all, you are the star performer—"

"—Oh Max, my darling," she interrupted swiftly, "that is a nice thought, but I am a performer, not a teacher. Besides, I cannot teach the girl something that comes to me so naturally."

Enthusiastic applause filled the theatre. Charlie skipped off stage, and the compere announced Monique de la Marre was about to appear.

"Please excuse me, Max. It is time for me to delight the crowd," the prima donna whispered before gliding onto the stage.

Max stood in the wings and watched the singer perform her much-loved repertoire. It was true that she had gained much popularity in London. The women paid particular attention to her beauty, while none of the men Max knew would have refused an invitation into her bed if they could keep it from their wives.

Thomas also watched Monique. He had worked with her for a long time, and he had never met anyone so beautiful and talented, and yet so nasty. The audience rose to their feet in appreciation of her imminent performance. They had applauded so loudly that Thomas could feel the floor vibrating beneath him. He wondered if they would still celebrate so much if they had been on the receiving end of her cruel streak. He, Max and David made their way behind the stage and off to the other set of wings to check everything was in order for Suzanna's debut at The Songbird.

Monique sang her last song of her show, a lively piece from a famous opera. It ended in a magnificent crescendo which demonstrated her powerful voice wonderfully. The audience were on their feet before the music died. The chanteuse wallowed in their admiration and congratulated herself on her stellar performance. *The newspaper columns are bound to give me a glowing review. Why wouldn't they? After all—I am, without doubt, the best singer in London.*

She made a beeline for Suzanna as she left the stage. David had a sense of foreboding and hurried off to intervene. Thomas and Max looked at the two ladies. It was clear from their body language that the diva was speaking at Suzanna and not to her.

"Max, I do not think that she is encouraging Suzanna."

"Fear not, David is with her now, Thomas, and she will be fine with him. Suzanna has great courage. Don't underestimate her."

Thomas smiled. Max was ever the optimist.

David was disgusted by Monique's behaviour. As he stood quietly in the shadows, his eyes were riveted on Suzanna. She seemed terrified, wringing her hands over and over while she waited for her turn to perform. He moved over to Suzanna and stood at her side.

Despite the angst contorting her face, to David, Suzanna looked beautiful. The little girl who had followed him everywhere had definitely become an elegant lady, and he could not take his eyes off her.

"Don't be afraid, Suzanna," he said gently.

She turned her head and looked into his bright blue eyes.

"I should never have agreed to do this," she muttered and hid her face in her hands.

"I have an idea," he said reassuringly. "Don't sing for the audience—sing for me. Forget about them. Focus on me in your mind's eye. I will be looking at you, encouraging you from afar. Trust me, you'll be fine."

She nodded, doing her utmost to compose herself.

"I have heard you practising with Mr Hoffman, and I believe in you," he said as he softly lowered her hands then tilted her chin towards him, his blue eyes boring into her soul.

She nodded again, still too anxious to answer him verbally.

"Go on, Suzanna," he urged, " I am here, right behind you. I will not leave this spot."

Suzanna closed her eyes for a few seconds, took a deep breath and then gave him a dazzling smile. She squeezed his hand as she lowered it from her face, and in turn, he pushed her forward.

"Go on, my girl, break their hearts. I believe in you."

Alas, despite David's pep talk, Suzanna's confidence floundered as she stepped out onto the stage to a dismal ripple of weak applause. A couple of people in the audience walked out before she had even sung a note.

Since it would have been more of an embarrassment if she ran away, she stayed rooted to the spot. All she could think of was how unprofessional she must appear to the sophisticated audience, particularly after Monique's stellar performance earlier. If only Suzanna had known the extent of her talent, she would have spent more time perfecting her skill than paying attention to the nasty French woman.

Staring out into the inky-black auditorium, she heard a few dresses rustling and she could make out the shadows of dark figures leaving. The spotlight swung on her as the audience fell completely silent. Suzanna interpreted all these things as an indication of failure. It was time for her to fight off the terror that all artists face at one time or another, rejection. She remembered David's words and closed her eyes. She started to conjure up an image of his reassuring face in her mind, and the sound of his calming words in her ear: 'I believe in you.'

Now in the limelight, Suzanna was emblazoned with a warm golden glow. Her white dress twinkled with shiny sequins and beads and made her look like an angel. Although the dress was spectacular, it did not detract from Suzanna's natural beauty. It was stylish without being provocative—unlike Monique's stage outfits with the daring low-cut bodices.

Her long hair hung to her waist and was tucked back with combs that her mother Maria had proudly given her. Her rich and exotic Gypsy features which she had inherited from her father, contrasted with the white dress, ensuring that she was the focus of the performance, and not her clothing.

Suzanna heard the orchestra shuffle in the pit, and she watched Conductor Hoffman raise the baton. The first bars of a haunting melody flooded the theatre. With perfect timing, she began to sing the opening line of the soulful song. Thankfully, those members of the audience who had considered leaving remained seated. Others who were waiting in the foyer for their coaches crept back into the theatre. From the instant that Suzanna opened her mouth to sing, she forgot her fear and became the music and the song. Unlike Monique, there was no provocative parading, no suggestion and no attempt at showmanship, yet, her understated performance had the audience in the palm of her hand.

Suzanna heard no applause for five long seconds after she stopped singing. *That's it. I have failed.* Then, in one collective movement, the audience rose to their feet and gave a thunderous ovation. There were shouts of bravo and demands for an encore. The atmosphere was one of celebration and the delight of discovering a new performer to enjoy. Old favourites on stage were always popular, of course, but a breath of fresh air was welcome too.

The novice singer was taken aback by the reception. She didn't know it at the time, but it was something she would become accustomed to. Overwhelmed by the warm and heartfelt response from the crowd, tears welled up in her eyes, then she ran off the stage in a panic, straight into the comforting arms of David, who was smiling from ear to ear.

"What did I tell you? They love you," David laughed.

"I was so scared," she gasped, overcome with emotion.

"It's natural to be scared," he reassured, "It was your first proper public performance."

Suzanna looked up at him and smiled. This gentleness was a side of David that he seldom revealed, preferring to be hidden in an office behind a pile of books.

"Go, Suzanna. Go and find your mother and celebrate. I can feel in my bones that you are going to be very famous one day."

"Thank you," she replied earnestly. "I would not have had the courage to walk out there if it hadn't been for you."

David smiled and squeezed her arm. Suzanna realised that David was his father's son. He was as kind as Max. *Just a little bit better at juggling the theatre's books, perhaps.* Back in the dressing room area, everyone congratulated Suzanna on her inauguration at The Songbird—except Monique. She intercepted the girl on her way to the sewing room.

"Now you are famous, oui? Just like that?" said Monique snapping her fingers in the air. "I do not think so. You have no talent little one," the diva continued. "They love you because you are so immature and inexperienced. They feel sentimental thinking back to their own children singing at home, clapping at the end of the song, come what may."

Peter stared at Monique, bitterly disappointed by her response to Suzanna's first-night success. Now the cheering had subsided, all Suzanna could hear in her mind was the hurtful criticism from the spiteful woman.

"Tomorrow, they will remember the poor child, not the voice, oui?" Monique continued. "Your heart will be broken when they forget

you, but do not be dismayed. It happens to so
many hopeful artists who fail to reach the
heights of fame."

Suzanna fled to her bed in the attic. Instead of pure joy
at her success, she now felt deflated and defeated. The
stinging pain from Monique's comments was all-
consuming. She was unable to console herself by
imagining that her bed was a golden gondola floating
under the Venetian bridges painted on the disused set
that surrounded her. In Suzanna's mind, she was a
failure.

She heard a soft knock on the door and, dejectedly stood
up to open it. As it creaked open, David came into view,
stood in the doorway with a large bunch of flowers.

"I thought you deserved these," he said,
smiling.

"And no, I did not steal them from Monique's
dressing room. I bought them from the
costermonger who sits in front of the theatre
at night."

Suzanna laughed and took the bouquet. She counted
two dozen enormous yellow roses. It was the first time
that she had ever received flowers, and she had no idea
how to react.

"Thank you," she said with a big smile, "I love
them."

And I love you, my dear Suzanna.

"You know I'll always be in the wings watching over you, I promise. You need never be afraid."

She nodded, innocent of the knowledge that he was no longer feeling brotherly love but was falling in love with her instead.

"The coach is waiting for us, you'd better hurry up."

Suzanna looked confused.

"Coach?"

"Yes. Did you think that I was joking when I told Monique that I was taking you to The Ritz?"

"Err, yes. Oh my!" she chirruped with delight at the idea.

"Hurry up, or they won't feed us," prompted David with a chuckle.

5

THE MEAL AT THE RITZ

The Ritz sparkled like a bright gem in the heart of Piccadilly. David's coach stopped at the front entrance, and he escorted Suzanna through the arched gates and into the luxurious hotel. Suzanna did not know what to concentrate on first. There was so much to see. The premises were full of late-night revellers who had come for dinner or drinks. Almost everybody recognised David as Max Liebowitz's son, and those who had been at The Songbird for the evening recognised Suzanna as the beautiful young singer who had stolen the show. Their eyes followed the couple as David led his guest to their seats at a quiet table for two.

Sitting at a crowded table nearby were Mademoiselle Monique and Lord Ashwood, surrounded by her fawning admirers. Earlier, The Ritz juddered to a discreet halt when Monique arrived. People loitering in the foyer flooded into the dining room to say that they had eaten in the same hall as the famous singer. Peter often wondered why she had never risen further and gone onto a more luxurious and lucrative life in Germany or Austria. Still, he consoled himself with the idea that he would never have met her if she had not focused her sights on London.

As David steered Suzanna to her seat, Monique did not notice the pair until the last minute. Even then, she pretended not to see them. As they passed by Peter Ashwood, he stood up to shake David's hand and offer Suzanna congratulations on her successful debut. Suzanna smiled, and her face lit up. David watched her with delight. He was so proud of her. After witnessing her the ordeal at the Crown, the success was all the sweeter.

"Suzanna made her stunning debut at The Songbird tonight, and she is the new talk of the town," toasted Peter Ashwood graciously. "Let us raise a glass to the lovely lady."

Monique looked at him through narrow eyes, and her face reddened under the powder. Ashwood saw her expression and ignored it. Monique was an ungracious loser at the best of times. The two singers' styles and acts were very different. In his mind, there was no need for jealousy to boil over. Monique, however, did not share that opinion.

The crowded table got to their feet, chinked their glasses together in celebration, then applauded softly. The men bowed and the women offered congratulations. Fuming and side-lined, Monique was no longer the centre of attention, and she could not bear it.

"Thank you," answered Suzanna sincerely.

"We were in the audience, Suzanna my dear," one of Monique's entourage blurted out, "and I must tell you that we were caught completely off guard. It is the best performance we have seen in a long time. Your angelic voice tugged at our heartstrings when you started your opening song. Then, you had us rolling in the aisles with your version of Marie Lloyd's 'What Did She Know About the Railways?' You have excelled on your first night."

Monique sneered at the man, wishing she could put her steak knife through his ribs to silence him.

"She was terrified at first," David explained. "She didn't believe me when I said that she has talent."

"I hope that you're going to perform regularly, Suzanna. Max won't be able to keep the crowds at bay."

Monique laughed, desperate to be the centre of attention once more. Getting up, she went to stand next to Suzanna, and wrapper her floaty feather boa around both their necks in an attempt to feign sisterly love.

"I am so happy that my protégé has followed in my footsteps. Together, Suzanna and I will fill The Songbird every night. Then, I might retire to Italy."

"Italy?" an admirer piped up.

Everyone turned to look at Monique for clarification.

"My dear, you cannot possibly leave us!" whined the voice.

Monique's smug smile confirmed she felt the centre of attention once again. David, however, was determined not to let her steal Suzanna's moment of glory.

"Suzanna will be singing regularly now, considering that she is our new 'songbird'. Since you enjoyed this evening so much, I am sure my father would be delighted to offer you free tickets to her next solo concert."

"Suzanna is going to have a concert?" Monique sneered at David incredulously.

"Of course, my dear," he whispered with a Cheshire cat smile.

"How dare you!" Monique hissed under her breath.

"No, Monique! How dare you. Stay away from Suzanna. Don't poison her with your bad character."

Peter watched the exchange between David and Monique. He did not know what David Liebowitz was telling her, but by the look on Monique's face, it wasn't going down well.

"Would you like to join us, David?" asked Peter, ever the gentleman, trying to smooth things over between the warring factions.

"We don't wish to intrude, Peter. But thank you for the invitation."

Peter watched them walk away. The dark-skinned girl was exquisite. He looked at Monique, covered in powder from forehead to bosom and he compared her to Suzanna, fresh and natural. Peter was beginning to have doubts over his feelings for his beloved famous fiancée. *She might be able to charm an audience, but she is becoming far less charming to me.*

"Are you enjoying yourself, Suzanna?" David enquired with a hopeful smile.

"Yes, of course! We should come here more often. As long as you are paying!"

David laughed at her.

"It's a deal. Every time you have a standing ovation, I will bring you here."

"But we will be here every night? We'll end up as fat as foie gras geese," she teased.

"Ah, yes. I didn't think of that, did I? I will be broke and you will be as round as a Christmas pudding!" David joked before they broke into fits of giggles.

David could not put his finger on it, but something had definitely changed between them. There was a curious tension between them that had never been there before. The two young friends were noticing that romantic love was slowly replacing the familiar, familial tie they used to feel. However, neither wanted to act upon their secret urge for fear of losing their lifelong friendship.

Suzanna was in awe of her surroundings. She had never been to such a sophisticated hotel, and she was overwhelmed by the beauty of it. There were beautifully shaped mirrors on all the walls, and the most delicate regency furniture filled the rooms. The carpet in the dining room was plush, and she could feel her feet sink into the pile. The chairs were upholstered in fine regency striped upholstery that matched the voluminous curtains and swagged pelmets. Large Christmas trees lined the hallways, decorated with rich red and gold glass kugels. Swathes of holly and ivy were tastefully wound around the pillars, studded with the latest fashion—small electrical lights that twinkled brightly. Together, the decorations created a magical atmosphere.

"Would you like to come here for cocktails on Christmas Day?" asked David.

"Oh, that would be lovely," she nodded in delight.

"Well, so be it! It'll be a nice way to round off a busy year."

It was well past midnight when they returned to The Songbird. He walked her up the stairs to her attic room, and she made him tea while he lounged on one of the tattered chaises.

"Thank you, David. Tonight was the most wonderful night of my life. My first proper performance on stage, the glorious meal, and your company. It was simply delightful."

"Perhaps it will be the first of many such nights?" he enquired with a hopeful tone.

Embarrassed by his forthrightness, Suzanna blushed and looked away. Eager to change the subject, David looked at his pocket watch.

"Don't worry about the tea, and I need to retire for the night. It is past my bedtime!"

"I don't want you to go yet. The night is still young!"

"I know, neither do I. But in the morning, we'll be dead to the world, and I am sure Max will have more errands for us."

David walked to the door and she followed him.

"Goodnight. Sleep tight," he whispered, leaning in a little towards her ear.

"Goodnight," she replied.

Before she knew it, he had leant forward and kissed her on the lips. It was the first time she had been kissed. Her heart galloped and thumped inside her. She prayed he would not hear it knocking against her ribs. With that he smiled and slipped away, blowing her another kiss as he closed the door behind him.

David left the theatre and walked across the road to his townhouse apartment. As he slipped off his shoes and collapsed into his Chesterfield armchair, he looked through the window and saw that Suzanna's light was already off. But Suzanna wasn't asleep. As the stage set of Venice surrounded her bed, in her mind's eye, she floated under the Bridge of Sighs in her golden gondola. Her mother had told her the legend that if a couple kissed while drifting underneath it at sunset, as the bells of St Mark's Campanile rang out, they would enjoy eternal love and happiness. As she imagined reclining in the ornate gold boat with the blissful image of David Liebowitz centre-stage in her thoughts, Suzanna made a wish that one day she would fall asleep in his protective arms—in real life.

6

SHE'S THE ONE

It was Monday morning, and David leaned back in his chair and looked at the pile of ledgers in front of him. For the first time in his career that he had no desire to work. All he wanted to do was sit back and dream about Suzanna. He was not sure what had happened to him or why his feelings towards her had become so romantic. One thing was for sure, without Suzanna at his side, his life was dull and empty. He decided it could only mean one thing—he was falling in love.

That Saturday night was the first time in years that he felt truly alive, simply because he had encouraged Suzanna to follow her lifelong dream. He had lived vicariously through her joyous moment. *Perhaps, my father feels this way when he makes somebody smile too.* He began to have more empathy with his father's propensity to put other people's happiness before his own financial wellbeing. Suddenly, his father's generosity and nurturing outlook made sense.

David threw his pen onto the desk, causing the ink to splatter everywhere. He sighed as he tried to blot the splotches away, then stood up and stretched. *Surely, there are better things to do on a Monday morning.* His mind wandered back and forth between Suzanna and the pile of work on his desk. Eventually, he gave up and focused on Suzanna.

As a young man, David had felt a vague affection for the occasional woman that he met, mostly when he was away studying at college. Still, this feeling for Suzanna was unlike anything that he had experienced before. He could think of nothing else except the soft skin of her cheek against his lips and an overwhelming desire to protect her. He did not believe that she was weak. On the contrary, she had worked with his cantankerous and unpredictable father longer than anyone else, which was proof of her mettle.

The lovestruck man put on his hat and coat and went to look for Thomas. When he found him, he was in deep conversation with Max.

"Come on, Papa, Tom, let us go and drink tea at Claridge's."

Thomas looked at David, suspiciously.

"Don't you have work to do? Your desk was covered in a thick layer of white when I saw it last—and it wasn't snow!"

"Of course, my desk is still stacked with paperwork. It's a never-ending battle."

"And you still want to go out? I don't think you have ever been out during working hours in all the years you've been doing The Songbird's books. Are you feeling alright?" joked Max.

"Well, are you coming with me or not?" demanded David.

"Yes. Yes. Let me get my coat, it's bitter outside," grumbled Thomas.

"And you, Papa?" snapped David.

"Of course, I am coming with you. It's not every day that my son falls in love!"

David frowned at his father. *How had the old goat guessed his news?* Fortunately, the comment seemed to fly over Thomas' head.

The three men arrived at Claridge's and were seated in the magnificent sitting room. The chairs were beautifully carved and polished. The walls were white with gold wall sconces. The staff had set the table with perfection in mind. The silverware was polished until you could see your face in it more clearly than a looking glass. The white tablecloths were crisp and elegantly draped with not a crease or crumb in sight. The linen, made with the finest Egyptian cotton, offset the delicate porcelain tableware and sparkling crystal glasses.

"Have you two forgotten about Christmas?" Max asked once they were seated.

David grunted, and Thomas sighed because they both knew how important Christmas was to Max. It seemed his Polish blood made him determined to bring endless yuletide cheer to his audiences in the cold depths of winter.

"I have been giving the festive programme, some thought. As you know, I am retiring soon, and I want to make this the best Christmas show that we have hosted in the history of The Songbird."

David and Thomas nodded in trepidation. For the past five years, each December Max said he was going to retire. Yet, the older man carried on working, tirelessly, making sure each Christmas was even more lavish than the previous year. David was already doing calculations in his head as to how he would finance the extravagance that Max insisted upon. Thomas was trying to imagine what sort of fantastic spectacle would need to be dreamed up this year.

"Not only am I retiring, but it is the last Christmas of this century. On Christmas Day, 1899, I will manage my last performance."

"Papa, The Songbird will never be a success without you."

"Of course it will, David, I have taught you and Thomas everything that I have learned in all my years of being the owner."

They both shook their heads, wondering how they would cope without Max. It might be an exhausting task to try to reign his enthusiastic plans, but Max Liebowitz certainly had a special connection with the crowd and empathy that David and Thomas's more clinical approaches lacked. The old thespian seemed able to read their minds.

"All you need to do to be successful is to have extravagant ideas and make them happen."

The two men groaned. Max was as undeterred as ever in the face of ruinous financial adversity.

"Now, you two, listen up. Over the years I have challenged you, David, to make plans for every eventuality with a minimal budget—" He paused to smile. "—and Thomas, I have taught you to create a magnificent show out of very few resources. What more training do you need?"

The two men said nothing and resigned themselves to bending to the patriarch's will once more—somehow, they would make his dream come true.

"So, what do you have in mind for Christmas this year?" Thomas enquired.

"I intend to create the greatest spectacle that the West End has ever seen."

"Yes, you always say that, but we need specifics. We can't start preparing if we don't know your plans."

"Well, two weeks before Christmas we will have a gala dedicated to the elite who have supported us for many years. Then, on Christmas Day," Max told them, "we will be entertaining the poorest of the poor—for free."

"So, there will be no paying customers on Christmas Day? I know you like to be charitable, Papa, but the theatre's finances are stretched to breaking point," exploded David.

"—And, in the spirit of the season, we will be offering them a festive meal and a glass of something to warm their cockles as well."

"Tell me you're joking, Max," said a worried Thomas.

"For heaven's sake, you two. We will have plenty of food. I am sure we can eke it out with some clever cooking. I can ask if our brewery suppliers might donate something to raise a little cheer—"

"—Even so," interrupted David, "I don't know how we will pay for it. Free entertainment for those who have fallen on hard times is one thing, but throwing in a hearty meal as well?

Well, this is the most ridiculous request you have made in years."

"My son, I have faith in you. You have never let me down. You will find a way. "

"What will you need me to do, Max?" Thomas wondered out loud.

"It is simple, my good fellow."

From experience, Thomas knew that it would be anything but simple. He anticipated the worst, and rightly so.

"I want Norway Fir spruce trees, the biggest trees that we can find. They have to decorate every nook and cranny," enthused Max, his eyes twinkling and his speech animated. "I want a lot of holly wreaths—with luscious red berries. And of course, there must be lots of lights that sparkle like stars. There must be big bunches of mistletoe under every arch."

Thomas and David's eyes grew wider as the list of requirements lengthened at a frightening pace.

"And we must dress up the entire theatre in the traditional Christmas colours of red, green and gold."

So far, Max had not mentioned any logistics that Thomas had not accomplished before—after a lengthy struggle, mind you.

"There shall be entertainment for every single person in attendance on Christmas Day. We will perform a full show for them."

David stared at him, startled.

"Father, your goodwill is beyond measure, but the cost—"

"—Oh, stop talking about money all the time," laughed Max. "You need to appreciate that this will probably be the first and only show that many of those people will ever experience in a real theatre in their lifetimes. We will provide a Christmas they will remember forever. And for that reason, so shall we."

David threw his hands up in the air and exhaled loudly.

"It's impossible. We simply don't have enough money to do both nights. You'll have to pick one or the other, Papa," the son wailed in desperation.

"No. You need to find the money," said Max with determination, "because I want to reward all the people who have blessed me over the years. Without them, I would be nothing."

"How have these poor people ever blessed you? You don't even know who they are!" protested Thomas.

Max was becoming annoyed with the two men.

"Yes, I do. And so do you!"

They looked at him agog.

"How?" David replied dismissively.

"Every single person who has ever delivered food to our premises, or fixed our coaches, painted our sets, sewed our stage outfits, painted the walls, fixed the floors, sold us flowers, swept the pavements outside and cleaned our floors inside—they have all helped us run our business. These hard-working men and women have received a pittance from their masters, and we need to acknowledge them. Without the workers, and their loyalty and labour, we would never have been as successful as we are."

Tired of arguing about money, David said nothing. His father would never accept how precarious their financial situation was as long as he lived. The only option was to limit the damage.

"Thomas," continued Max, "Find Lee Ting-Chong. I want the best Chinese fireworks."

David's heart sank. *Fireworks! Please not indoors! He's getting worse in his old age!*

Thomas' anxiety levels also lept sky high, but for a different reason. He had never arranged fireworks before and was terrified of them burning down the building. The newspapers were always full of calamitous events involving fiery showpieces backfiring on stage. Mishaps were common.

"Also, before I forget, I have spoken to Lord Ashwood. He is providing all the pheasants we need for the Christmas Gala dinner for our wealthy supporters."

David nodded with relief at the news. It was the first sensible thing that Max had said since they sat down.

"Ashwood has one condition, though," warned Max. "We have to spend a weekend at his country house and hunt them ourselves."

David could not believe what he was hearing. He was a city gent through and through, and country pursuits were outside his remit and experience—not that Max was bothered about such details. The frustrated son chose to stare out of the window and dream about Suzanna instead. Seconds later, he was dragged back to the grim reality of the planning.

"How are we going to raise the finances for the event, David? Tell me what cunning scheme you were hatching just then," demanded Max in excitement.

"There is no cunning scheme. I have no idea how we will fund—"

The son's words of concern fell on deaf ears as Max's liveliness heightened further. Once the old man got a bee in his bonnet about a kind gesture he wanted to make, there was little that could be done to stop him.

"I want all the regular Christmas fayre throughout the season: Pheasant, ham, turkey, vegetables, potatoes. Yorkshire pudding with gravy, plum pudding and custard. And mince pies—plenty of those. The cook can bake those in advance. They'll keep fresh for days in tins. Large bowls of punch and mulled wine would be lovely and warming. And trifle—with sherry in it, of course. Have I missed anything?" Max asked as he raised his eyebrows.

"Christmas cake?" advised Thomas despondently.

"Of course, yes! Christmas cake. How silly of me to forget! We'll need dozens of those," roared Max in delight as he imagined more details of the festivities and the sea of happy faces enjoying them. "Can we stretch to a sixpence in the cake, or will you killjoys begrudge me that little bit of extra expenditure, too?"

"For goodness sake, Papa! All we ask is that you be realistic with your plans. By all means, have fun, just cut your cloth to your means."

David's voice trailed off as he realised he was wasting his breath. The tea and cake arrived, and the three men ate in silence. David and Thomas were too terrified to say another word in case Max thought of something else to add to the burgeoning list of requirements.

It was Thomas who came up with the solution while he was finishing his cup of Earl Grey. He began to grin.

"What is it?" demanded David, struggling to see anything to smile about.

"I have the perfect resolution to this little financial conundrum."

Max was bouncing around with glee. David thought Thomas might be losing his grip on reality even more than his father. Thomas cleared his throat as he dabbed his lips dry with a crisp white napkin.

"Gentlemen, we are going to have a competition on the gala night—a singing competition between Suzanna and Monique. Monique will draw her usual huge crowds of wealthy patrons. We can double the entry fee for this unique extravaganza. Why? Because two weeks before Christmas everyone has a looser grip on their purse strings. We'll easily bankroll the Christmas Day event."

It was the worst idea that David had ever heard. As he sighed, he let his eyelids droop down to shield him from the nightmare scenario that was emerging before him.

He imagined Max and Thomas like massive snowballs rolling down a steep hill, hurtling further out of control, gathering pace and power with every second they were left unattended. The metaphor was exactly how he saw the Christmas project was turning out. *Bedlam.*

"Yes! By Jove, that is pure genius!" exclaimed Max. "Gentlemen, this Christmas competition will be the talk of the town. Anyone who is anyone will be itching to attend. Get onto the newspaper forthwith, Thomas. We need to advertise it. Well done, my man, I couldn't have thought of a better idea myself."

7

LET BATTLE COMMENCE

Early the next morning, Max called Monique and Suzanna to the stage. He never dealt with the performers in his office, believing that addressing them from behind his desk was cold and intimidating. Rapport with his performers mattered.

"Beautiful ladies," Max began. "I realised that we have considerable talent in our humble establishment. Therefore, I have decided that we will hold a singing competition on our annual gala night. The tickets sold will raise money for our charitable luncheon on Christmas Day. I can guarantee the glorious prize will make it a very special evening for one of you."

The two women looked baffled. Both the competition and the luncheon were news to them.

"Yesterday, I went to the Italian Embassy, to pull a few strings with my friend the ambassador. He's agreed that the best singer on the night will get a chance to audition for the Florence opera at Teatro Verdi," Max continued. "The winner will depart for Italy shortly after, and off to the chance of a lifetime."

AN excited Max had been busy planning the competition since the meeting at Claridge's the day before.

"C'est vrai?" Monique crooned in her delightful French accent. "Magnifique! It will be a dream come true for me," she added presumptuously.

Suzanna flinched at the gravity of Max's news and Monique's arrogant response to it.

"The ambassador, Francesco de Renzis, and his wife will attend. He will deliver the opening speech and announce the winner. It will be a wonderful evening. Anyone who is anyone will want to be there. We will certainly top up the theatre's coffers. And ladies, imagine the opportunity to study and perform at the greatest opera house in the world."

Monique gasped in fake humility and sincere delight.

"Choose your songs carefully. It goes without saying, you should add several soprano solos to your set to make the best impression you can," Max instructed them. "I am thrilled. I cannot think of a better way to begin my retirement."

"I can't wait to start planning my act," chirruped the starlet.

With all of Monique's experience and crowd-pleasing talent, Max was confident that the diva would win. Nevertheless, he thought it was kinder to give his loyal assistant Suzanna her moment in the limelight instead of sourcing another celebrity singer on the variety circuit. *It will be good for her soul and give her confidence in the future. And she can always take over from Monique when she leaves.* Motionless, Suzanna was still stunned.

"Thank you for the opportunity, Max. Please excuse me, I have lots of errands to attend to."

The young girl scuttled away, glad to be free of the daunting peacocking presence of Monique.

"Oh, Max, this is excellent, oui!" Monique enthused. "I have waited for this moment since I was a child. I had started to believe that I may never have the opportunity to join such a prestigious institution. I have dreamed of working on the continent for years."

"Good luck, my dear. You have served me well over the years, and I wanted to repay you in some way before I hand the business over to

David and Thomas. I hope your wish will come true at last. Of course, it will be a great loss to The Songbird—"

"—and it will be a great loss to the Florence opera if they do not choose me," mused Monique in her own selfish little world.

"Of course, dear," muttered Max, looking crestfallen at her display of ingratitude.

"Oh, Max! You are making me feel guilty, oui! Still, it is time to follow my dream, and it will be such a compliment to be recognised for my outstanding talent."

Max listened to Monique, hoping that Suzanna had the same confidence. Even if Monique was rude and impetuous, she could afford to be. She had an incredible voice that lifted the roof off the theatre, and the necessary beauty and stage presence that accompanied successful starlets.

"Well done, Monique, you deserve it. But don't take it for granted that you will be chosen. You still need to triumph over Suzanna on the night."

"Of course I will," she replied haughtily, "very few singers can compete with Mademoiselle de la Marre."

*

Browsing his burgeoning to-do list, Thomas decided to take a cab to St. Giles to look for Lee Ting-Chong, the fireworks specialist. Max had given him some vague directions to a Chinese laundry in the roughest part of the city. After searching street after street, a weary Thomas finally reached his destination. He opened the door and could hear the nattering of Chinese women standing beside large bubbling cauldrons of murky grey water with clouds of steam billowing from them. The heat and humidity were beyond unbearable, and Thomas wondered how people could work in that environment all day.

"Lee no here," said the eldest of the ladies.

Thomas frowned at the thought of his fraught, wasted journey.

"Lee gone tea loom," she added with a smile.

"Where is the tearoom?" he asked.

"Tea loom in Whitechapel," she said, smiling and nodding away but not really helping since Whitechapel was awash with tea rooms.

A young lady came over. She spoke better English, so Thomas asked her the same question.

"No, no. Mister. Not Whitechapel. He gone tearoom Westminster."

"Do you have a name of the street?"

"No. Very sorry, Mister."

Thomas had no choice but to take a cab to Westminster and take potluck. After trudging up and down almost every street, he spotted the tiniest tea shop that might fit the bill. Above the door, a red sign wafted on its wrought iron hanging. The establishment's name was written in gold Chinese lettering. For all, he knew it could have said 'Down with British Government!' but he hoped it said 'tea shop'.

Thomas darted to the tiny entrance, opened the faded black door, stooped down and stepped into a dark room lit by a mass of red paper lanterns hanging from the low ceiling. They swung at the same height as his head, forcing him to dodge them as he tried to find his way to a promising-looking table where six Chinese men played Mahjong.

"You look for Lee Ting-Chong?"

He nodded.

"Lee not here. He go to Wapping. Look for Red Dragon."

Thomas sighed, hailed a cab and proceeded back towards to the docks, not that far from where he first began his search.

"Red Dragon," Thomas instructed the coachman as he yanked the cab door open.

"Bloody hell, mate! What is a nice geezer like you wanting with a dive like the Red Dragon?"

"Why?" asked Thomas, "I've never been to the place. Is it dangerous?"

"You could say that," answered the cabbie. "It's a Chinese brothel."

"Wonderful," muttered Thomas woefully as he climbed inside.

The Red Dragon would have provided a thorough education for many a young man who did not know his way about the female anatomy. Thomas had to do his best to ignore the naked and semi-naked women milling about the rooms and corridors. The brothel stood in a derelict building beside the most rundown dockyard in the area. Before he was allowed into the house, Thomas had to convince the Chinese bouncer lingering by the entrance steps that he was not a policeman.

Max's harassed aide climbed a winding staircase and eventually popped up on a landing that had more red Chinese lanterns hanging from every rafter. They created a soft warm glow in the corridors adjoining the rooms where the bawdy entertainment took place. The low diffused light also disguised the dilapidated condition of the venue.

Thomas' search stopped abruptly when a no-nonsense Chinese man approached.

"You want girl? We have lovely girl. Cheap."

Thomas shook his head.

"I'm looking for Lee Ting Chong."

"Why you look for Lee? Who your boss now?"

"Max Liebowitz," Thomas replied.

"Aaah! Yes, Mr Max. I know Max, good man. Come, I take you to Lee."

"Lee," the Chinaman called out. "Here man from Mr Max," and as he began to prattle off in Mandarin, Thomas's eyes glazed over.

Lee stood up and walked to greet his visitor. He had been sitting around a table drinking whisky out of a tiny porcelain teacup with dainty pagodas in blue and black hand painted on it. Lee looked at the design and then smiled as he revealed his motive for using it.

"Aaah, when police come, we say we only drink tea. Nothing to see here. We good boys," Lee said earnestly.

Thomas chortled to himself thinking it wouldn't fool a copper for a minute.

"Why Mr Max want me come to him?"

"He's looking for fireworks. Don't ask me what he has in mind though," Thomas explained wearily. "They are for our Christmas shows."

"Ah-ha," said Lee with a smile. "We make fireworks—big fireworks. Much bang— bang—bang! And lots of light! Process not easy though. It takes much skill. We can help make big success for Mr Max. People will 'ooh' and 'ahh', I promise!"

"Do you need anything from us?" asked Thomas.

"Gunpowder. Mr Max must give us much gunpowder, then we make."

"Heavens!" exclaimed Thomas, "Where the hell do I find gunpowder?"

"Velly simple. Mr Max must ask army man. Then we make for you at Singing Bird."

"You mean 'The Songbird.'" corrected Thomas with a frown.

"Yes, that's it, Singing Bird."

Thomas did not have the energy to correct Lee a second time.

"I bring family. We work in attic. Many hands work velly quick. We do good job for Mr Max."

The aide could not believe what he was hearing. *David is never going to agree to Lee's plan to do the manufacturing on the premises. What if Lee and his family blow up the theatre during their preparations? What is Max getting us into this time?* Not wanting to disappoint his employer, against his better judgement, Thomas nodded at the cheerful little Chinese man, confirming his acceptance of the offer.

"Yes, please do bring all your household. You will be most welcome. Max needs the fireworks as soon as possible."

Two days later, Lee arrived at The Songbird with his sizeable family in toe. Thomas counted twenty-six people. More than half of them were children. At the tail end of the queue of people, there was a hunched up old woman with hands so gnarled and swollen from arthritis that Thomas wondered if she had any dexterity for work at all.

"What are the children going to do all day?" asked Thomas, having terrible visions of them running around the place.

"They work," said Lee merrily.

"Yes, but doing what?"

"They make firework. We all make firework. Not granny, though. She cook."

"We will provide food for you. There's no need to worry about that," Thomas volunteered worried that open cooking flames and barrels of gunpowder were not a good mix.

"We not like your English food. Granny Chong will cook in your kitchen, Mr Thomas"

"Erm—yes, alright."

As the strange collection of workers trouped along the corridors and up to their rooms in the attic, Thomas laughed loudly and the absurdity of it all. David was right about The Songbird being a circus—especially now.

"Mr Thomas? Why you laugh? What funny?"

"Oh, nothing, Mr Lee. You carry on, my good fellow."

8

HABANERA

Monique began practising her operatic repertoire from the moment she heard about the competition. Her powerful voice wafted through the building. Even though she could be a selfish shrew at times, Suzanna could not deny that the woman was a consummate professional who worked hard to progress her career and deserved all her success. The feisty diva's commitment, years of experience, and legions of loyal fans began to cast deep shadows in the young girl's mind.

"David, I am not up to this competition. I am bound to be humiliated. They need to find another singer to compete to make it a fair fight. Only a few weeks ago, the audience threw pint glasses at my head to get me to leave the stage!"

"How many times do I have to say the debacle at The Crown and Cushion was not a reflection of your ability. Do you really want to give someone else the opportunity and then spend the rest of your life regretting that you never even tried?" he quizzed. "The last time you trod the boards here your act was well-received. You know that. It's time to forget your nerves and put your heart and soul into your performance. Do you not think the whole audience will be rooting for the underdog? It's so terribly British—unlike Monique," he said with a chuckle.

Suzanna smiled at the joke hoping she looked more positive, even if she didn't feel it. Monique was a formidable opponent in every way imaginable.

Several times during her morning practice, Monique had lost her temper with the orchestra and yelled at the conductor.

"Amateurs!" she screamed. "You are all amateurs, oui! You are not fit to perform in the sewers of Paris."

"Mademoiselle," ordered Hoffman, "please take five minutes to calm down. Have a drink, perhaps. We will begin again when your temper has subsided."

Monique stomped off like a self-interested toddler. Hoffman had been mistreated for months, and he was close to throwing down his baton and taking the orchestra with him. When Max came to see what the commotion was, Hoffman voiced his concerns.

"I am telling you, Max, Monique is impossible. If I did not respect you, I would leave this instant. She can sing accompanied by a honky-tonk pianist for all I care—if there is one stupid enough to work with her."

"I know she is difficult," Max agreed, "but she will be leaving us as soon as she wins this competition. Her profile is on the up, you know that. You have to admit that she has brought us fame and fortune," Max reasoned diplomatically. "We owe her this opportunity."

"I suppose making her look good at the gala will be the same as writing her a glowing reference to tempt a foolish employer to take her off our hands," he mused.

"You are a professional, Mr Hoffman, and Monique is a diva. That is the hand we have been dealt. Please have as much patience with her as you can. We need the gala to be a success to raise the maximum amount of money. If Monique pulls out, those hungry bellies at Christmas Day will be on your conscience."

"The woman is a selfish ungrateful French shrew. The sooner she leaves for Italy the better. I am warning you, Max, everyone has

had enough of her petulant antics. Either she
goes, or we go. I am sure The Canterbury
Theatre will want our services."

At times like this, Max wished David was there to
witness the day-to-day challenges that he faced. The old
man's naturally empathetic outlook meant he was left to
reconcile the warring factions. Max was under a
constant barrage of pressure to compliment, console,
manipulate and encourage an endless string of over-
emotional performers who believed that the world
revolved around them.

He had enjoyed a long theatrical career, and he loved his
life, yet as the years went by, he found he had less
patience left for the selfish people that surrounded him
and sapped him of his energy. Although he was a
wealthy and generous man, for many years now, he
never had time for a woman. He wanted to escape the
chaos and find someone whom he could enjoy life with,
a woman who would spoil him in his twilight years. *I've
been alone for far too long now.*

In a rare moment of calm, Mr Hoffman spotted Suzanna
sitting in the gallery.

"Err—Miss Stratton! Why are you up there?
Come here at once."

She glided down the stairs, her simple linen dress
flowing behind her, skipped through the foyer and
across to the empty auditorium. As she walked down
the left aisle, the conductor questioned her.

"Wouldn't you like to practise a little? The competition is only a few days away," reminded Mr Hoffman. "What were you doing up there anyway?"

Suzanna climbed the wooden steps to the side of the stage and took up a central position above the orchestra pit, then turned to face the conductor.

"I was watching Monique perform. She is magnificent," Suzanna eulogised politely.

Despairing sighs emanated from the orchestra pit.

"What are you singing at the gala night? We have not discussed it yet. Have you chosen something?"

"Yes, Mr Hoffman," she answered shyly.

"Well spit it out, Suzanna. We cannot help you if you do not tell us."

"I am going to sing Habanera, from Bizet's Carmen."

Mr Hoffman's mouth opened and then shut again. It had been on the tip of his tongue to refuse her and ask her to choose something less ambitious, but on reflection, he thought she should at least try.

"Do you believe that you have the tonality and the vocal range?"

"Yes, I have been practising."

"How so? Where did you get the sheet music? Can you read music?"

"I went to Denmark Street and bought the sheet music with my earnings. I have practised the piano since I was a child. I seldom mention it, but there have been many musicians who taught me through the years."

Mr Hoffman stared at her in pride and wonderment. *A working-class girl who has the drive to teach herself the piano definitely needs this opportunity to prove herself.*

"Bring me the music and meet me here in thirty minutes once the orchestra has had a run-through of it," he instructed her.

"Yes, Sir. But what about Monique? Has she finished practising yet?"

"Monique can wait until tomorrow. I have had enough of her antics for one day."

"I presume you're not expecting me to break the news to her!" said Suzanna in a panic.

"I'll deal with the situation," sighed the battle-weary musician.

Monique stood in the wings, eavesdropping on the conversation between the conductor and Suzanna. She was furious. *How dare that man speak about me in that manner.* Still, as arrogant as she was, she realised that if she annoyed the conductor any further, he would refuse to work with her. Although it was a fractious relationship, they had worked together for countless performances. Changing to a new conductor now could ruin her Italian adventure.

From what Monique overheard, her first challenge would be to salvage the relationship with the musicians. She hatched a plan. She would return to the stage and charm Mr Hoffman and his orchestra until she was once again the 'darling of the theatre'. *I'll tell them a little white lie that they can work with me on an all-expenses-paid tour of the continent too, just to be sure I win them over.* Her second challenge was to find a position in the shadows where she could hear Suzanna make a fool of herself as she warbled her way through 'Habanera'. With a smug grin, Monique decided both challenges were easy to achieve.

Monique made her way up to the balcony. Her strategic position was well-chosen. She chose the door closest to the stage and placed herself in the shadows. From there, she could look down on the orchestra and watch closely Suzanna as well. *This delicate English rose will never manage to do justice to the gritty anthem of a passionate Spaniard like Carmen.*

The orchestra began to play a few bars into the introduction, and Suzanna began to sing. A hush fell over the entire building. Stagehands, costume designers, cleaners and cooks arrived in dribs and drabs to watch the young woman perform the song of Carmen the Gypsy, hoping they would not get called back to work. The song seemed as if it were written for Suzanna.

She reached all of the high notes and pronounced the words perfectly, even though they were not in her mother tongue.

Monique was so distracted by Suzanna's delivery that she did not see the staff slipping into the auditorium one at a time. Even Lee Ting-Chong 's family were amazed. David stood watching from the wings, wholly absorbed in the song. Everyone saw Suzanna and yet they didn't. Her committed performance had transformed her into the embodiment of Bizet's Carmen. It was clear, once again, she had the ability to capture the heart and soul of her audience.

As the song ended and Suzanna looked forward into the darkness, the orchestra jumped to their feet and applauded. Her co-workers swarmed onto the stage to congratulate her. Maria and the other seamstresses watched her, all filled with pride. Suzanna did not understand the irony of the song she had chosen, but Maria did. The excitement subsided, and everybody scuttled back to their work before Max found them away from their posts.

Suzanna saw David walking down the central aisle toward her. He skipped up the stage steps two at a time.

"How did you do that, Suzanna?" he asked with pride and admiration in his voice.

"I did what you told me to."

"What was that?" he asked, puzzled.

"I imagined your face and I sang to you," she whispered.

David didn't respond to the comment, and Suzanna felt slighted. She regretted the comment instantly.

"It's time to get back to work, I think," he said, coolly. "I'll explain more on the way back to the office."

Her heart sank. Her moment of glory was over far too soon. As they walked into the wings, David took her hand and pulled her toward him. He put one hand around her waist and the other behind her back. Gently he drew her towards him. It was the second time that David had kissed her, and this time he did not stop. It was deliciously long and lingering. Eventually, they parted, relieved no one had seen them.

"You were magnificent. Truly magnificent!" he gushed.

Suzanna was speechless.

"May I bring you flowers tonight and come for tea?"

"Of course," she said with a smile.

"Oh, and you don't need to come back to the office just yet, that was just my way of getting you alone. Go and enjoy your moment of triumph with your mother."

Cheekily, he smiled over his shoulder as he walked towards the backstage door. Suzanna was smitten. *He's adorable.*

After watching Suzanna's performance, Monique felt fear and fury. It was the best performance she had seen in quite some time. She knew that her French refinement would inhibit her from performing with such raw passion. There was a real danger this young nobody would supersede The Songbird's resident headline act. The ego-bruised French starlet choked back her tears and ran to her room, careful to avoid bumping into anyone along the way. She threw herself upon her antique bed and sobbed. Burying her head deeply into her thick feather pillow, she silenced her cries. There in the soft blackness, she imagined Suzanna, stood amid her enraptured co-workers, humbled and embarrassed.

Max and Thomas were sitting in David's office as he returned.

"Did you hear Suzanna's performance, David?" asked Max

"Yes, I did."

"We need to find a place for her to study music," muttered Max with a frown.

David did not respond. The thought of her leaving had not crossed his mind—until now. His throat tightened with stress. He was glad his father continued the conversation, else he feared he would have been unable to make a sound.

"She has lived in this theatre since she was a child, and her mother has been loyal. They are more like family than employees. I would like to help if I can."

"Perhaps, we can contact the Royal School of Music," pondered Thomas.

"Possibly. I don't think that the typical British musical hall goer will appreciate Suzanna's classical repertoire. They are looking for the bawdy acts such as Marie Lloyd these days, not opera."

"I expect we'll need to send her abroad, just like Monique if she is to develop her voice for the soprano solos."

"Father, can I please take care of this after Christmas? At the moment, everything is a challenge."

Max smiled, noticing that lovestruck David was looking glum.

"Yes, that is a good idea. Let's leave it for now and focus on tonight's performance. It's only a few hours until the curtain goes up."

David could not wait for that evening's show to end. The days that used to go by in a flash had now become long and tedious. Much as he hated to admit it, the time spent away from Suzanna dragged. The first thing that he was going to do when his father retired was appoint a new accountant to take over his soul-sapping role. In the last week, he realised that a life spent battling with bookkeeping was meaningless.

He made his way to the attic, accompanied by old Granny Chong, who was holding a tray with a massive bowl of noodles in a questionable watery broth. Beside the bowl was a pot of green tea. David put out his hands in an offer to help. Granny Chong, not used to chivalry, pulled the tray towards her making it slosh about dangerously. Muttering something incoherent in Mandarin, he feared she might be invoking an ancient Chinese curse. The old woman watched him with a scowl as he knocked on Suzanna's door.

"Come in quickly," she told him, "Mrs Chong and Mrs Bowles, the cook, have struck up an unlikely friendship, and they will gossip about us."

David took the tray off Granny Chong and shooed her away. Suzanna closed the door behind him, He looked around her room and smiled, noticing the change of set.

"When I brought you flowers last time you were living in Venice," he teased her.

"Yes, last night I moved to Paris."

Now, her bed stood beside a screen painted with the Arc de Triomphe. In the distance was the Eifel Tower.

Suzanna had propped up another screen which showed a small street café. Next to that, she had rounded up four rickety French-looking chairs and a small table. In the corner was the battered and thread-bare chaise longue. David was pleased to note she had put his yellow roses into a vase and placed them next to her bed where she could see and smell them. They seemed to be holding up remarkably well with not a dropped petal or wizened leaf in sight.

He stood next to her while she made tea. He studied her smooth amber skin and smouldering eyes. Her dark hair framed her beautiful features. She had the appearance of a slender flamenco dancer. He wanted to kiss her delicate neck but resisted. His anxious mind returned to the possibility that the competition night would be the last time he would see her. He wanted to protect her, even though she seemed to be a thoroughly modern young woman. *Or perhaps I want to protect myself from the pain of letting her go.*

9

SUNDATARA

The next day, Max sauntered into Thomas' office, did a little dance at the door then twirled on the spot, emulating the comedian Champagne Charlie. Thomas braced himself. Whenever Max was excited it was an ominous sign he was about to share another one of his bright ideas.

"I have been at the docks this morning, Thomas, and I encountered the most interesting people and things there," Max revealed earnestly.

"Do I need to call David?" asked Thomas.

"Not yet—I am afraid that my new idea will incur his wrath. Let me tell you first."

Thomas lifted an eyebrow. Max wanting to avoid David was another bad sign.

"There were some Hindi people at the dock. They're delivering an elephant to a travelling circus from up north."

"No, Max," said Thomas putting his hands up defensively. "I have heard enough. I know what you're going to say. It's a terrible idea. I can understand why you're scared to tell David."

"Hang on before you dismiss the idea. They don't want payment for the elephant, Thomas. They are prepared to lend her to us for nothing," Max protested. "And one of their chaps is a snake charmer too. Has a wicker basket with a deadly cobra in it, apparently. Imagine what an interesting addition that would be to the Christmas show. Our very own menagerie. It used to be such a draw at the Tower of London in the sixteen hundreds! The Songbird will bring that old tradition back to life here on our stage!"

Thomas stood up and opened the door. He disappeared for a minute and returned with David. With a concerned look, they both sat down. Thomas sighed then began to fill David in with the latest bold scheme Max had dreamed up.

"He has met some Hindi people at the docks. They want to lend him an elephant for the show, and there is a snake charmer available as well, so he says."

David rolled his eyes in despair.

"No, Papa. Definitely not. Do you have any idea how much food is needed to sustain a fully grown elephant? And the idea of deadly cobras escaping in the auditorium in front of a live audience doesn't bear thinking about. What do these people really want from you?"

"They are not just 'these people', David. Stop being so dismissive. It's such an ugly trait of yours. They are a family in a bit of a fix—and you know how I feel about families experiencing hardship. Unsurprisingly, Mr Thakur, who hails from Bombay, is struggling to find his feet and feed his family now he is thousands of miles from home. They are delivering the elephant to a travelling circus, but they have nowhere to keep her before then. The skipper is sailing back to India soon and the beast needs to be off the boat. The circus is travelling down from Nottingham after Goose Fair, so Mr Thakur says."

"Father, do you even know if our tired old wooden stage can support the weight of a fully grown elephant?"

"Probably. I can confirm that with the carpenter. It has supported two dozen chorus girls doing the Can-Can with not so much as a creak. Stop fretting, David."

"And this Indian family, now the ship has docked, I expect they will need a place to live as well, will they?"

"Well, err—yes," Max informed his son sheepishly.

An enraged David thumped the desk with his fist and gave Thomas a wide-eyed and beleaguered look.

"Now, David, don't overreact. The last thing I need is another person behaving insufferably."

"What do you mean by that, Max?" argued Thomas, angry their loyalty was being questioned.

The pent-up frustration of managing the staff finally got the better of Max and unburdened his soul.

"Well, where shall I start? Monique is ready to relive the Battle of Waterloo with Suzanna, and she vows that this time the French will win. Granny Chong is a vicious little woman who hisses at me whenever I am close to her despite me giving her a place to live. Mr Hoffman, the conductor, is threatening to up and leave with the orchestra and go to The Canterbury if Monique does not stop her nonsense," he argued. "What's more, in the loft is a gaggle of Chinese waifs and strays who are turning twenty barrels of highly-explosive gunpowder supplied by the British Army into fireworks."

"Heavens above!" exclaimed David. "You hadn't told me about the gunpowder, Papa. I thought those barrels were empty—props for our production of HMS Pinafore. Twenty barrels of gunpowder secretly squirrelled away in the building will make Guy Fawkes look like an amateur. You will blow up all of the West End if something amiss happens."

"It's perfectly safe. Mr Lee is a professional. The Chinese have been using gunpowder for thousands of years. There really is no need to worry."

David was too exhausted to argue. This time he relied on Thomas to put his foot down on his behalf.

"If the police find out about all that gunpowder, Max, you will end up in gaol. I know we needed a small quantity for a controlled display, but twenty barrels is utter madness. What were you thinking?"

"It is for a good cause, Thomas. I want to retire with a bang."

"It will be more than that—it will be a bang that takes the bloody roof off."

"And the Thakur family?" asked Max, "What am I going to tell them? We have to take them in else they will end up in Whitechapel and be murdered. Do you want that on your conscience? Because I don't!"

"How big is their family?" asked Thomas.

"There are fourteen altogether, seven children and seven adults," said Max meekly, hoping it would sound less of an imposition.

"Glory be, Max! And let's not forget the homeless elephant and snake. I know we have plenty of space here, but that's not the point. It is a working theatre, not a hostel for the needy. To my reckoning, between the Thakurs and the Ting-Chong family, there are forty people that you are happy to take in?" asked Thomas.

"Yes," said Max, convinced that the matter was settled.

"No!" roared David as he re-entered the conversation, unable to bite his tongue any longer.

He shouted so loudly that Thomas and Max jumped.

"Enough! There is a plethora of little Chinese children running around. I found them swinging from the ropes backstage and doing somersaults off the sets. We'll be in the papers if one of the little oiks breaks his neck. Then what will you do, Papa?"

His concerns went unheeded. Max's mind was already elsewhere.

"Hmm—they have acrobatic talent? Perhaps we can use them in the show?"

Thomas and David were apoplectic at the unconcerned comment. If Max had been a younger man, they might have lynched him. Thankfully, the trio's escalating hostilities were interrupted by a knock on the door.

"Come in," called David.

Mrs Bowles appeared.

"I am sorry to interrupt. An Indian family is asking for you, Max."

"Ah, thank you, Mrs Bowles. So, they have arrived safely."

"Yes, Max, fourteen of 'em. Out of the blue. I don't suppose they'll manage on fresh air. They'll eat us out of house and home," she grumbled

Max rushed out of the office to welcome his new friends. The children were already sitting at the kitchen table drinking sweet tea and rapidly working their way through a pile of biscuits, like a plague of locusts stripping a crop. The women were dressed in bright elegant saris that swished around them as they walked. They looked so exotic. The men seemed to be relaxed as their wives and children chattered away like noisy birds.

"Mrs Bowles, find somebody to take the Thakur family up to the attic if you would be so kind. There are some prop storerooms next to the Chong family. It's not ideal, but at least they will be comfortable there. They managed to live cheek-by-jowl on the ship on their long passage, so it will feel very spacious in comparison. I'll ask the stagehands to empty it for you."

Max gave Mrs Bowles a weak smile as he felt her angry eyes bore into him, then called Mr Thakur aside.

"I have arranged that we move 'Sundatara' tomorrow night. I hope that the local constables will turn a blind eye. We will have to keep her well-hidden. Everything must happen after dark. We don't have a permit to keep her here just yet, but that is a mere formality, I'm sure."

"What will we feed her, Max?" asked Mr Thakur. "She has a huge appetite and will strip

and eat the leaves, twigs and bark off a large
tree every day. We only have a few bags of
food left from the trip."

Deep in thought Max put his hands in his pockets and
looked into the courtyard. Moments later, a look of relief
appeared on his face.

"We are accepting a delivery of our Christmas
trees tomorrow. What a remarkable
coincidence. I am sure there will be more than
enough to decorate the theatre and ensure
that Sundatara has a square meal. We'll only
be stealing one a day from the display, so no
one will even notice."

"Not to start with, at least," joked Mr Thakur.
"You must remember to take the decorations
off first, Mr Leibowitz. I don't suppose she will
appreciate those."

Elsewhere in the theatre, Thomas knocked on David's
office door and let himself in.

As usual, David's desk housed a stack of letters and bills.
The ledgers and journals were piled high, and the eagle-
eyed accountant was lounging with his feet on the desk.
Thomas had never seen him more despondent.

"Why does he insist on overruling us with
these crazy ideas? It's like he lacks any
common sense. At his ripe old age too? He

says it's my mother's influence. She's been gone for years though!"

"Come, old boy," reassured Thomas. "We've been through worse with him."

"Have we? Each Christmas his plans get more farfetched."

"Yes, I suppose you're right. They broke the mould when they made Max."

David started to chuckle. He took his hanky from his pocket and waved it in the air.

"I surrender, Thomas," he jested. "Pour us a drink, will you? I am not sure I can take much more of this chaos."

Thomas reached into the bottom drawer of the tall filing cabinet and pulled out a bottle of whisky and two cut-crystal tumblers.

"Needs must," he said as he poured out the large measures.

"Indeed," David replied as he snatched the glass out of his colleague's hand. "Down the hatch!"

Thomas poured two with more with a grin.

"Medicinal, old chap. I prescribe a four-finger dose. That should fix you."

A little later, there was a loud and urgent knock on the door. It was Mrs Bowles on another firefighting mission.

"David, Thomas, we have a problem with Granny Thakur this time."

Thomas looked at her with a familiar expression she knew to mean 'what now?' David covered his eyes in anticipation of what was to come.

"Granny Thakur refuses to eat my English meals. She wants to cook her food in our staff kitchen. We need all the space available to prepare for Christmas."

Thomas put his head in his hands. David looked at him and began to laugh then Thomas began to snigger too. Mrs Bowles slammed the door in annoyance because she thought that the tipsy pair were both laughing at her, rather than helping.

"Come on, David! You're slacking," noted Thomas. "Clearly, two drinks will not be enough to get us through the day."

*

David Liebowitz had taken the back stairs hoping to avoid any people, but by the time he reached the second floor, he was ambushed by seven little Hindi children who were sliding down the bannisters. He had caught them in the act of mischief and glared angrily. They looked at him with big sad eyes. As if by magic, they transformed themselves from little horrors into the most innocent little angels. He wished that Max had been there to witness their antics—he would have wanted to use them in his show too.

Hearing the shuffle of light footsteps, he glanced behind him. They were following him up the staircase to Susanna's room in the attic. David thought that if he ignored them, they would go away, but they stalked him to the top of the stairs and made no secret that they wanted to see who he was visiting. *Trying to be discreet is doomed in this place.* He shooed them away with a wide sweep of his arm, then took a deep breath and knocked despite his misgivings that he was still being watched.

"I have a message from my father about tonight's show," David announced loudly, hoping it would put their inquisitive minds at rest.

"Well you'd better come in," she said with a smile.

David stretched out on the chaise and patted the cushion.

"Come and sit with me."

Suzanna nervously obliged. David gently pulled her toward him until she lay comfortably in his arms with her head resting on his chest. He felt her soft body against his broad torso and stroked her long hair. He studied her lovely face and admired her wild Gypsy looks, concluding that she was as exquisite as ever. *Not only can she out-sing Monique de la Marre, but she is more beautiful too—inside and out.*

She turned her face up to look at him, and he kissed her. It was clear to the pair that any thoughts of the sibling love they used to share was gone. She removed his tie and undid the first three buttons of his shirt and slid her soft hand under the crisp white fabric, caressing his bare skin with her fingertips. Instinctively, he slid his hand down towards her hips then stopped himself. Suzanna was surprised when he pulled his hand away.

He fidgeted as he fastened his shirt buttons and knotted his tie.

"I am sorry, Suzanna. I have gone too far."

"Not against my will," she replied. "I am not offended if that's what's worrying you?"

She sank back against his chest to show she was at ease in his company, and, with torn emotions, he pulled her towards him once more. David kissed her hair tenderly then sighed as he turned his head away.

"Something is weighing heavily on my mind, Suzanna."

"What is it? You can tell me," she reassured, softly tilting his face towards her with her hand.

David decided blurting out his worries was the best approach.

"Suzanna, what will you do if you are chosen for the Florence Opera?"

"I haven't given it any thought," she laughed. "I am not expecting to win the competition, let alone succeed at the audition stage."

"There is always a possibility that you will. You don't know what the judges are looking for. They might have a specific role in mind— a role you might be perfectly suited for."

"I won't lie. It would be a dream come true for me," she confessed. "To be taught in Italy would be such a great honour. If I win the competition and turn down the opportunity to go to Florence, I will always regret it," she said, echoing David's opinion.

David lay quietly, enjoying the pleasure that he derived from her innocent touch. Deep down in his heart though, he suspected that there was no future for them. *I must break this off before it goes too far.*

Something in his marrow told him that Suzanna was going to win the contest and leave him behind to follow her dreams as she built a life for herself. *Soon, I will be nothing but a fond memory. Perhaps when she achieves fame, she will come back to me? It can be lonely at the top, so they say?*

As soon as he thought they might be together, he doubted it. *Why would she leave a career in Florence for me?* Minute by minute, he was losing his heart to somebody who would never be his, and there was nothing he could do about it. Despite the obvious mutual attraction, he was not selfish, and would not make her choose between him and her dreams. *Suzanna is a strong woman. She doesn't need to be in love. It is better for her career if she has no distractions and no guilt.*

"I have to leave," he whispered, reckoning this
to be the last time that he would visit her
room alone.

"I'll see you tomorrow, won't I?" she said as
she gazed fondly into his eyes.

With their faces mere inches apart, both unable to resist, David pulled her into his arms and kissed her passionately, then felt repentant. *Why do I succumb so easily? This has to stop.*

He snuck out of her room, hoping not to bump into the attendees of the newly formed Liebowitz kindergarten on the stairs.

10

SEARCHING FOR SID PAYNE

Thomas reached the slums of St. Giles later than he had hoped. His departure from The Songbird was delayed by a lively dispute that broke out between the Hindu and the Chinese families.

One of the Hindi children had slipped and fallen as a group of them were sliding down the bannisters. The Hindi lad accused a Chinese boy of pushing him and a nasty scuffle broke out. The matter escalated into a violent altercation, which in turn lead to the two fiercely protective grannies stepping in to protect their wards. Anarchy reigned. Fists flailed wildly to an accompaniment of screams and yelps. While the two older women fought to save their family honour, the two children had already made friends again and were back to having fun swinging on the ropes behind the stage.

Mrs Bowles had sent Thomas to separate the boisterous elders. The two women only called a truce when he threatened to put them out on the street. Granny Thakur went into her room, muttering something in Hindi as she slammed the door and Granny Chong yelled something in Mandarin and waved her fist above her head.

"Will you please try and calm down, all of you!" Max bellowed up the stairs, losing his relaxed demeanour for once. "Thomas, get down here—now!" he ordered.

The young man bounded down the stairs, looking perturbed. He was regretting peeking around the door to check on the Chinese workers. The vision within of them sitting around large piles of loose gunpowder as they scooped it carefully into tubes made his blood pressure leap sky-high.

"What is it now, Max?" snapped Thomas.

"I want you to get to St. Giles, pronto. Something urgent has been brought to my attention."

"St. Giles! But why?"

"We are being proactive in our Christmas preparations."

"We are?" said the aide, looking stunned.

"We've never been organised at Christmas ever! It's always been done by the seat of our pants."

"Look, I haven't got time to argue, Thomas. I want you to find a man called Sergeant Payne. He's a former soldier. Served in India in the artillery division. He's an expert about all things to do with the sub-continent. We will need assistance keeping Sundatara under control," the flustered old man explained.

"What is 'Sundatara'?"

"Who, not what, Thomas. Pay attention. I told you about her already. Sundatara is the fully-grown female elephant who is under Mr Thakur's guardianship."

"Do you have an address for Sergeant Payne? Perhaps I should make enquiries at the local police station?"

"Have you got cloth ears today, Thomas? Payne is an army sergeant, not a bobby. Do keep up," Max sighed. "He frequents 'Sally's Pub'."

"That sounds rather like a brothel, Max!"

"Perhaps it is," Max replied uneasily, "but you will find him there. He is a regular—when he's not here. Oh, and you might need this for cab fares, or information."

Max thrust some cash into Thomas' hands. He swallowed hard as he looked down at the money. There was quite a lot of it and Thomas wondered what he was getting himself into.

"Right, then. I'll be off, boss."

Reluctantly, Thomas shoved the cash into his coat pocket then plodded off slowly towards the backstage door.

"And be quick about it! There are more
errands to attend to when you get back!"
badgered Max.

Thomas took the short cab ride into St. Giles. Along with Whitechapel, he thought it was the worst place to be stuck in after dark. He looked out of the window hoping his mission would be quick to complete. The thought of getting garrotted for his pocket watch as he traipsed around looking for an amateur elephant handler he'd never met before made his nerves jangle.

After unpinning his watch-chain, he tucked his prized timepiece into his inside pocket, then did up the coat buttons to make sure it was well hidden.

His efforts were seemingly pointless. As soon as he hopped out of the cab, he would be a target. Only wealthy people could afford to travel in style. The poor had to make do with the bone-shaking omnibus. Worse still, Thomas had little practical experience navigating the challenges of the grimy thoroughfares of London on foot. His naivety was apparent as he paid the cab driver.

He whipped out the wad of notes that Max had given him—in full view of everybody on the street.

A local scallywag called Danny was eagerly eyeing the newcomer from the street corner. He nodded to Paddy, his Irish sidekick, a ruthless rogue from Belfast, who was hidden in a dark, narrow alleyway opposite.

Danny sidled up to Thomas and smiled at him with all the charm he could muster.

"Do yer need some help there, mate?" the scoundrel enquired.

"Yes, please," answered Thomas politely. "I am looking for Sally's Bar. I have to meet a friend there."

"I bet you do," sneered Danny greedily as he thought about the rich pickings on offer before he remembered he needed to earn Thomas's trust to get to the cash. "Danny Ripley at your service, Sir!" he said, transforming his demeanour in a flash.

Thomas was delighted he had found someone so helpful so quickly.

"Now, let me think," chirped Danny cheerfully. "Yeah, now I remember. Take that narrow street across the way there, squire. Keep going, then make a left when you see the foundry. At the end of that road, a sharp right will get you to Sally's."

"Is it far?" asked Thomas.

"No, mate. Just a couple of minutes, that's all."

"Thank you kindly."

The newcomer doffed his cap, impressed that the ragged-looking man had been so helpful. *Everyone warned me about the area, but I cannot complain about my treatment so far.* Danny made a show of shaking Thomas's hand and waving him off.

Max's aide walked towards the narrow alleyway and confidently turned left when he got to the foundry. As he turned the next corner, someone hit him.

Thomas presumed he must have lost consciousness at some stage because when he came to, he had mysteriously developed a black eye, a nasty bump on the bridge of his nose and his ribs felt as if they had shattered and were piercing his chest when he breathed in. Hardly able to move, he had to crawl down to the end of the narrow alley to get his bearings.

Even in his injured state, he could not believe his eyes when he looked to the right. A few yards away from him was a small pub. He squinted at it with his good eye. The sign read, 'Sally's'. *That thug Danny pointed me in the right direction, at least—even if it was via his violent accomplice. How kind!* From then on, Thomas was on guard. Standing unaided was still out of the question, so he hid in the alley, leaning against the brick wall until he regained his strength.

There was a constant stream of people coming and going from Sally's establishment who walked past him as if he was invisible. Eventually, luck was on his side when a beautiful young woman noticed his bruised face, stopped and asked if she could be of assistance.

It was unlikely that he would be granted admission to Sally's in his current bloodied state, so he was relieved that she had taken an interest. *Perhaps she can look for Payne on my behalf.*

"Hello, sweetheart. My word, aren't you worse for wear? Been through the wars a bit, ain'tcha?"

Thomas nodded, feeling very sorry for himself. All he wanted was for her to pull him to her ample bosom and offer him shelter.

"How can I help you, fella?"

"I am looking for Sergeant Payne," Thomas replied, his chest burning like fire when he breathed in to speak. "Do you know him?"

"Of course I do, me angel!" she said with a great big smile. "Who can I say you are, sweetheart?"

"Tell him my name is Thomas. I am a friend of Max Liebowitz."

"You just stay right there now," she cooed reassuringly, "I will bring him over."

Thomas must have lost consciousness again because when he came to this time the woman had gone and a huge man was bending over him. The army chap was completely bald, yet he had a spectacular handlebar moustache that was waxed into position so robustly that the points almost reached his eyes. He was the most gigantic human that Thomas had ever encountered.

"Ouch," winced Sergeant Payne, when he saw the state of Thomas. "You are in a sorry state. That posh coat tells me you're not from round here, are ya lad? What has brought you to Sally's?"

"Sergeant Payne, I presume?" asked a bleary-eyed Thomas.

"Yes, Sir."

"Max Liebowitz at The Songbird has sent me to fetch you. We have an Indian elephant— Sundatara—that we need help with."

"A-ha," he exclaimed excitably, "So, where is the beauty?"

"She is on a ship at the docks. Max needs to move her to the theatre."

"Do the authorities know about this? There is a possibility that Sundatara will be a difficult woman if she gets startled. She might inflict an injury upon someone—which may be a bit tricky to explain away. Elephants can be quite temperamental, especially when they find themselves in unfamiliar surroundings."

"Max is convinced that you are the only person who can help him."

"Tell Mr Liebowitz that I will help him with pleasure. We're like brothers. Go back a long way, we do."

Thomas couldn't remember Max mentioning Payne before, but was in too much pain to care about the conundrum. He started to slide back down the wall as his knees buckled. Some gritty footsteps crunched over towards him.

"Let's get you on your feet, sweetheart," purred the beautiful woman in a surprisingly deep voice.

"He's in a dreadful mess, Lily," warned Payne. "He's in no shape to go anywhere. Looks like he's cracked a few ribs."

"Let's take him inside, get him patched up a bit, and make him comfortable, shall we, Sid?"

Sergeant Payne picked Thomas up effortlessly, carefully carried him up the stairs and lay him on a tatty-looking bed. Within seconds, six women were bending over the new arrival, discussing him as if he was not there.

"Yeah, they did a good number on him, Sarge," said one.

"Where's he from, Sid?" asked another.

"He works at The Songbird? You heard of it?"

"Aye. It's the theatre, in the West End. Posh, eh?" said a husky female voice.

Thomas heard Sergeant Payne's voice again.

"Ladies, can you patch him up and keep him here for the night? I will find him a cab in the morning and send him back to the theatre," advised Sid. "I doubt he will live to tell the tale of his adventures if we leave him to find his own way home tonight," he added with a laugh.

"Of course, Sarge. I presume there must be some reward in it for us?" asked Lily. "Playing nursemaid won't earn us a penny tonight."

"What do you want?" asked Thomas. "All the money I had with me has been stolen."

"Well, I heard something about a Christmas show."

Thomas nodded with a wince.

"I can get you tickets. How many do you need?"

"We don't want tickets, flower, we want a part in it!" proclaimed Lily, smiling broadly and revealing several toothless gaps.

The dazed man nodded his agreement, not really caring about the artistic or practical consequences of his decision. *Since they've gone out of their way to help me, Max would want it no other way, I'm sure of it.* Sid made his excuses and sloped off. The women offered to leave their patient to rest quietly for an hour mainly because it was a handy cover story for heading off downstairs for a few celebratory gins.

Thomas shuffled the lumpy pillows about with a pitiful groan then lay back on his side. No matter how he positioned himself something hurt. Two hours later, he heard loud cackling as the drunken women trooped back upstairs to resume their bedside vigil. It was going to be a long night.

11

'TIS THE SEASON TO BE JOLLY

It was late morning, and David noted he had still not seen Thomas, a man known for his punctual reliability, and he began to worry. The kitchen was the backstage hub for the theatre staff. Thomas had not been in to get a cuppa and no one remembered seeing him wandering about the courtyard either. By lunchtime, David was gravely concerned and went to ask if anybody had seen his right-hand man.

The place was overflowing with cooks and their underlings. The air was filled with the unmistakable smell of Christmas fayre, in particular, the rich spicy aroma of fruit mince steeped in brandy. The bakers were rolling out dough and creating tempting little pies that David could never resist.

Max was standing in the courtyard, eagerly accepting his huge consignment of Christmas trees. A poor labourer sweated profusely as he unloaded the delivery from his wooden wagon. As David approached his father, he heard Max order another two dozen from the chap.

"Papa, we don't need any more trees—we are awash with them! What are you thinking?"

"Ah, David, here you are. Yes, I have ordered more. There can never be too many trees. They are such a cost-effective way to brighten up the whole theatre, don't you think? I thought you would approve?" fibbed Max, knowing full well the bulk of them would become meals for Sundatara.

David looked around the courtyard. It resembled a dense Scandinavian forest. Even if Thomas only used half of them to decorate The Songbird, there would still be far too many. *My old man's up to something again. The question is what?*

"We won't be able to move for the damned things!" bellowed David in frustration. "No more, Papa. We need to keep the courtyard free for accepting all the other goods deliveries you've ordered."

"Of course, my boy. You're right," said Max, trying to flatter his son to calm him down.

"Do you know where Thomas is? I haven't seen him all morning?"

"I gave him some money and sent him to St. Giles to fetch a friend of mine," answered Max.

"This morning?"

"No, last night."

"And he isn't back yet?"

"I hope not," whispered Max behind his hand with a nudge and a wink.

David frowned, wanting more of an explanation.

"I sent him to find my friend Sergeant Payne who served in the 22nd regiment in India."

"Why?"

"I need Payne to look after Sundatara, of course," beamed Max.

"Sundatara—?"

"—that elephant of Mr Thakur's."

"Right," said David, regretting starting the conversation. "When are you fetching her from the docks?"

"Tonight. Very late tonight. Best to transport her under the cover of darkness. Sorting out the official permit to keep an exotic animal on the premises is proving tricky."

David did not argue. He knew it was pointless. Once Max's mind was made up about fun to be had, that was that. The sensible young man's logical head was spinning at the thought of the beast roaming around the theatre. He went off to the housekeeper's office for some peace and quiet.

"Sit down, David," Mrs Bowles suggested. "You seem terribly glum this morning?"

He gave her a feeble smile, then sank back into his world-weary countenance.

"Max is up to his usual over-the-top yuletide antics, Mrs Bowles."

"That's to be expected, lad," chuckled the cook.

"Hmm. There's another thing. Thomas went missing yesterday evening in St. Giles. I've only just been told. He's nowhere to be seen."

David was worried about Thomas. Like him, Thomas had enjoyed a sheltered upbringing and the ragamuffins on the wrong side of town would easily eat him alive. *What if he has been robbed? Or maybe he had his drink spiked and he frittered away Max's money on a night of hedonistic lust?* On top of those concerns, he felt bleak at the thought of losing Suzanna./

"Thomas is not your concern, David. He's a grown man who can look after himself."

"I suppose so. May I please have a cup of tea and once of your legendary mince pies, Mrs Bowles? That'll put a smile on my face."

"Of course you may. Let me get them for you, poppet. You sit and have a breather. This place at Christmas is enough to drive anyone round the bend."

David wolfed down the pie, but he still felt maudlin.

*

To David's relief, Thomas arrived late in the afternoon, accompanied by Sergeant Payne and an unusual bevy of noisy, scantily clad women.

"Welcome! Welcome!" cried Max when he saw the new arrivals.

"We have an injured soldier with us," said Payne. "Some thugs put the boot into him. He looks a mess, but he'll survive."

"Thomas," cried Max when he saw the battered young man and rushed to his side. "I am so sorry for sending you to such a dangerous place. I will never be able to erase this from my mind."

"You would have made a terrible general, Max," commented the army man. "Gotta get used to the rough and tumble of battle."

"I am fine, Max. I am," Thomas whimpered as he took a deep breath to continue. "I lost all your money. I asked for directions, and the gits sent me down an alleyway. I was like a sitting duck. They clobbered me all over, then took every penny that you gave me."

"Your life is more important to me than the money, Thomas. Never forget that."

"I do have quite a tale to tell now, though!" the aide added excitedly with a pained grin as he cracked his freshly scabbed lips open once more.

"Let's get him upstairs, Sid."

David reached the kitchen in time to see Max and Sergeant Payne manhandling the wounded assistant up the steps. He rushed to his friend's side and relieved his exhausted father.

"Let's take him to his barracks," said Payne. "He must return to active duty as quickly as possible."

"I'm just a bit stiff," countered Thomas not finding the military play-acting funny in the slightest. "When it wears off, I'll be fine."

"You are a fine, private. I'll make sure you get a mention in dispatches for your bravery."

Thomas looked baffled by Sid's response. David decided to take charge of the situation.

"Let's get you into a bath of hot water with some Epsom salts in it. You can soak your muscles. I am sure that it will help. You seem more bruised than grazed."

He looked at the female rabble that had descended on the kitchen.

"Who are all these ladies?" he asked Thomas.

"I was lucky they saved me. A girl called Lily found me after I was beaten up."

"Where are they from?"

"Sally's Bar," he answered. "And I promised them a part in the show because they saved my life."

"Of course, of course, what a wonderful idea, Thomas. I would have done precisely the same thing," roared the eavesdropping Max.

"What a pleasure to have you all here. Thank you for taking such good care of Mr Bartlett," gushed the old man. "Please, make yourselves at home and enjoy our hospitality."

David's frustration level soared. He pulled Max to one side.

"Where are they going to sleep, Father? We already have enough waifs and strays staying with us. They must return to St. Giles until the show. They have homes and they must return to them."

"Good grief, no! They must practice, David. And they need measuring for costumes. And then there are the fittings. I cannot have the seamstresses running back and forth to St. Giles. What if something happens to them? I almost sent poor old Thomas to his death, and I will not put my ladies in danger."

"Two dressing rooms are standing empty next to Monique's suite, and we have some cots in the basement," Max explained. "There is plenty of space. Sergeant Payne will sleep in the courtyard stable and keep an eye on Sundatara."

"Papa, we cannot fit another soul under this roof. Why you feel that you have to accommodate them?"

Max tutted in annoyance.

"David, imagine they took that 'I'm alright Jack' attitude with Thomas. He would be lying in a gutter dying in a slum. You need to show these people a little gratitude and have some humility and compassion. I expect better from you, I really do. This selfish streak of yours is most unbecoming."

David did not answer him back. It was on the tip of his tongue to chastise Max for sending Thomas into the horrid slum in the first place. However, he guessed that his father felt terrible enough already without an ear bashing from him, and so he let the matter rest.

"Look at them, David. Those women have nobody else but each other. Sergeant Payne was a man who bravely joined the army to fight for our queen and country. They might seem a little odd, but they are still a family, David, and you know how I love families."

*

It was past midnight when Sergeant Payne set out for the docks. His military mind had assembled a small platoon of soldiers to accompany him on the mission. Mr Thakur and his sons, a few stagehands and Max made up the small contingent. They had no experience in battle, but Sergeant Payne's forces background told him that under his skilled leadership, they would rise to the occasion.

"The most important thing is that Sundatara trusts us," explained Sid. "I had to travel into the city to buy these," he said, opening a large sack that contained lovely ripe clementines. "They cost me an arm and a leg, but ellies love 'em—so she is going to love me too."

As the posse reached the dark harbour, Max warned them that they only had a few hours before the dockyard became busy again and they were to be swift. Mr Thakur paced up the gangplank and found a watchman who was only too happy to release the terrifying creature into the Indian's care. Just a few pounds was all it took to buy the guard's silence. Mr Thakur beckoned the beast out of the ship's hold. All the men took a step back when they saw the huge elephant looming towards them. She was more of a mountain than a beast. Still, Sergeant Payne and Mr Thakur seemed fearless in her presence. Sid gazed at Sundatara with adoration in his eyes and Sundatara responded by putting her inquisitive trunk into the sack and helping herself to a juicy clementine. Max did not understand why Sid had brought so few men with him, because there would be no way they would be able to control the mighty Sundatara if they offended her. He hoped she remained placid.

In the light of a full moon, Max stared at the beautiful majestic animal, delighting in her beautiful eyes with their lush long lashes. *She was born to be a superstar.* Sundatara looked at Max and but quickly lost interest when Sergeant Payne, increasingly keen to get moving, seduced her with another delicious clementine. He took a few steps back, then waved another tempting fruit in the air, steering her slowly towards the dark streets that led to The Songbird. The massive beast's colossal feet softly padded down the winding lanes without making a sound.

Thirty minutes later, they found themselves one street away from the theatre. Sergeant Payne was about to congratulate himself on the successful mission when he saw a figure standing beside an alley. Sundatara and the platoon stopped in their tracks. The elephant began to flap her ears wildly, a sure sign that she did not appreciate a stranger standing in her path.

"Don't do anything rash," ordered Sergeant Payne through gritted teeth. "Keep calm. Sundatara is very sensitive. One sniff of panic will cause her to rampage through the streets."

Max's eyes grew big and wide. He had not anticipated wild rampages when they were planning the mission. He thought the beast would be placid and easily controlled with an expert handler like Sid. That was turning out not to be the case. The concerned animal's ears were turning into a blur they were moving so fast.

"It's a copper," hissed Sid.

The officer was walking toward them, determination in every step he took.

"Let me deal with this. Stay back," whispered Max.

"Alright, Max, but move slowly and speak softly. We don't know what to expect from the man—or Sundatara."

Sergeant Payne lectured his friend as if he were about to begin negotiations with an enraged cannibal in the heart of Africa, not a lone London bobby on his beat.

Max ambled forward to meet the policeman and shook his hand.

"Hello, Max! Nice night for a stroll, I see," said Constable Wilkin, looking at the strange sight before him.

"Hello there, officer. Season's greetings to you!" he replied in a friendly whisper.

"Well, I must say, I wasn't expecting to be starting my beat like this."

—Meaning?" said Max, playing dumb.

"Meaning what on earth are you doing processing through the streets with an elephant, Max?"

"Ah, this old girl is going to be a part of my yuletide show on Christmas Day," Max explained.

"The law regarding horse and carts is explicit about not harming people or property—but this—" Wilkins paused to collect his thoughts. "—I suppose the same rules apply. Although if I am not mistaken, an elephant is an exotic animal that belongs in a circus or zoo with a

trained handler, not a side street with you,
Max. Do you have a permit?"

"Constable, I have no other way of
transporting this beautiful lady, and I take full
responsibility for any damage she may cause
en route. As you can see, she is wonderfully
placid. And, we're nearly home now."

As he said that, Max hoped Sid Payne still had enough
clementines to hand, else they were going to be in deep
trouble. The theatre owner thought it was time for a
little white lie to get their operation swiftly underway
once more.

"The permit papers are in hand, I promise,
officer. Things have slowed down a bit with
people winding down for the festive holiday."

"Since I can't recall the specifics of a law
pertaining to elephants in transit, Sir, I
suggest you get her off the streets as soon as
possible."

"Of course, constable!" Max reassured. "Err,
why not bring the family over on Christmas
Day? Your children will love it to see
Sundatara perform before their very eyes,"
suggested Max hopefully.

Constable Wilkins tutted and shook his head
disparagingly.

"I do not take bribes, Mr Liebowitz."

"But, it's not a bribe, constable. We are inviting widows and orphans too. And, this year, the Christmas Day performance is completely free. My way of saying thanks to the community for all their support throughout the year. You in particular have done a marvellous job of keeping pickpockets away from our entrance."

"Well, that's different then, I suppose," said the policeman solemnly. "I will ask the missus and the kids if they want to go."

"Excellent! I do hope you can all make it," said Max, patting the officer firmly on the shoulder. "Let's move along, lads, shall we?" the old man urged.

"Yes," agreed Sergeant Payne. He moved his mouth close to Max's ear. "Sundatara is becoming grumpy. I am running out of clementines and her philosophy in life is, 'no food, no friendship'. We must get her stabled while I still have a few treats left."

"Good night, officer," said Max, as he nervously beckoned the party to follow him back to the theatre.

The band of men and the massive elephant marched into The Songbird's courtyard, the immense beast barely fitting through the archway usually reserved for carriages and delivery carts. Max was relieved to note that Sundatara soon settled in her new home and gleefully began stripping the bark off her first Christmas tree.

"I am sure there are no pine trees in India, but she's tucking into that spruce with gusto," Max cheered, delighted to see the animal happy.

Mr Thakur's boys gave the elephant's trunk a light stroke with their hands and wished her goodnight as their father made sure the heavy wooden doors to the courtyard were firmly shut. He didn't fancy the prospect of the beast breaking loose and having to explain to her rightful owners why he had lost her.

As things finally settled down, Max invited Sid to share a nightcap with him in his sitting room.

"I believe that the campaign was successful," said Payne importantly.

"Of course, it was! Congratulations are in order, old friend," said Max, raising his glass to the military man. "Your leadership was commendable."

"Thank you, Sir. Tonight's mission was highly successful—we suffered no casualties and achieved our objective."

Max found Sid's quirky turn of phrase amusing. The two friends were no longer young men. The excitement of the night had tired them both, and the brandy had numbed their exhausted minds. Within minutes of settling in their plush armchairs, Max was in a trance, staring into the fire on the edge of sleep. Sergeant Payne's eyes were already closed, and he was snoring softly, glass at a precarious angle in his hand.

*

The first noise sounded like a quick roll of thunder. Initially, Max ignored it until he remembered the moonlit sky during their procession earlier. Suddenly, there was an almighty explosion that rocked the building. Sergeant Payne jumped to attention.

"Cannon fire!" he roared.

Max looked on, mystified. The former soldier's eyes darted around the room looking for a rifle. Thankfully, Max did not have one or, in the confusion, it might have caused a greater calamity. Sergeant Payne settled for a thick iron poker, and then in his addled mind loaded it in anticipation of a confrontation. With his strange behaviour and outbursts, Max was beginning to wonder if his dear friend was suffering from shellshock or some other mental infirmity. The next observation confirmed Max's suspicions. Sid ordered an imaginary army into an attacking formation.

"All men to their battle stations! Follow me, boys!"

Sergeant Payne took to the stairs at a rapid pace, heading toward the sound of the cannon fire with only a nervous Max following him. By the time they reached the top floor, Lee Ting-Chong was already standing in the corridor, wearing his pure-white long johns.

"Me solly"! Me so solly, Mr Max!" he cried.

"What the hell is going on here?" demanded Sergeant Payne, "You have been surrounded. Give up your weapons. Surrender at once!"

Payne was holding the poker and aiming it at Lee as he would a standard-issue army rifle.

"Where is the general?" demanded the Sergeant.

"No general! No war!" stammered Lee.

Sergeant Payne kept the poker aimed at the Chinaman's head.

"No shoot me. I will 'splain bomb," begged Lee.

In a moment of brilliance, Lee bent over and took off his long Johns. He held them in the air and waved them as if he were surrendering.

"You cannot trick me, sonny Jim," snarled Sid. "I won't lower this weapon until you convince me there is no bomb."

Menacingly, Sid raised the poker above his head, a prime position to cleave his opponent's skull with a single blow. Lee was cowering, covering his manhood with bunched up long-johns. A mob of little Chinese children were behind him, laughing at his naked derrière. Other people who had made the theatre their impromptu home crowded onto the landing to see what all the ruckus was about.

Max, in desperation, tried to resolve the situation before it got any worse.

"Stand down, Sergeant!" he ordered in a stern voice. "The enemy has surrendered."

Sergeant Payne lowered his weapon. Lee was hysterical, having almost lost his life to a lunatic aiming a metal poker at his head.

"No bomb, Max. Granny Chong light match for cigarette. Granny drop match. Match light firework fuse. Me throw firework high up, out of window. Big bang in sky, not bang building! We safe!" said Lee.

"Well, it seems there is no damage done," said Max in relief, surprised at how well he reacted to Lee's tale.

Max and Sid rushed to the window and looked out. All they could see were tiny pieces of paper fluttering high up in the air, now slowly sinking to the ground.

David heard the blast in his flat across the road from The Songbird. He bolted from his bed and ran to the window and yanked open the curtains. He could see a light way up in Lee's attic room, and then saw his father and Sergeant Payne staring through the window in awe. The young man watched as copious quantities of ash fell like grey snow, covering everything in its path. *What if the rest of the fireworks go off!*

The explosion had woken up everybody in the street. Mortified, David watched his neighbours open their windows to see what was happening outside. He took a quick pace back and pulled the drapes firmly closed to shut out the unfolding crisis—and ease his nerves.

Curiosity getting the better of him, David pulled on his clothes and ran across the street like a mad man. The foremost thing on his mind was ensuring that Suzanna was safe. He banged his fist on the locked courtyard doors and demanded to be let in. Mr Thakur obliged. Blinkered with concern for his woman's welfare, David rushed across the courtyard, taking no notice of the Thakur boys efforts to calm the distressed elephant. He flung the stage door open with a deafening crash.

He shot up the back staircase to the attic and shoved his way through the extended Songbird family. He did not care who saw him or what they thought. *I need to know she's safe.* With palpable relief, he saw Suzanna observing all the excitement, her face lit up with joy as the humorous spectacle unfolded. David grabbed her arm and pulled her away.

"Come with me," was the whispered order.

"I'm in no danger," she said, yanking her arm free.

"I don't care. I don't want you in this place, with all these lunatics."

The young Chinese boys had tired of sniggering at Mr Lee and were running around the legs of Max and Sargent Payne, playing tig. Granny Chong was becoming worryingly defensive again.

"I suppose you have a point, David," she conceded.

Quickly, they made their way to his apartment, with David glancing at his neighbours' curtains hoping to see fewer twitching open than before.

Upstairs, David slid his fingertips between his window drapes and looked through the tiniest sliver of a gap he could manage. He waited for five minutes to see if any flames were coming from the theatre. One loose spark could spell disaster if it landed on one of the wooden eaves, but thankfully there were none. He closed the curtain praying that there wouldn't be more disasters at The Songbird before dawn.

"What a night!" said Suzanna, as she collapsed into a fireside chair in fits of giggles, which continued as she filled David in with all the amusing details.

12

ESCAPING THE CHAOS

Suzanna's eyes began to droop, and she gave a deep sigh followed by a yawn. It was well past everyone's bedtime.

"You are sleeping here tonight. I won't have you in that disaster zone over there."

"But there's only one bed, David?"

"Just think of it like sharing with your mother. No one will know. I need to get some rest before I speak to my father tomorrow. Goodness knows how I am going to resolve this situation. Those fireworks on the premises are an accident waiting to happen."

He went to the bathroom and slipped into his cotton nightshirt, then climbed in next to Suzanna, making sure none of his body touched hers. She looked a little shocked at his forwardness, but appreciated it was the most practical solution under the circumstances. David was obviously shattered and dealing with Max was going to take considerable effort. *A good night's sleep will help them both.*

Suzanna fell asleep immediately, but David could not. Just as he closed his eyes, he thought he heard the loud trumpeting of an elephant, but decided his exhausted mind was playing tricks on him. In the morning, he would discover it wasn't.

He could not take his eyes off her peaceful face as he felt her body heat warming the bed up. All he wanted to do was put his arms around her and wake her up, but he bit his tongue and lay there, motionless, observing her.

Suzanna rolled over in her sleep and sighed. By now, the temptation was too great. He kissed her lightly on her forehead, put his arm around her waist and gently manoeuvred his body up against hers. Dozing and barely awake, instinctively, she put her arm over him. His fingertips could feel her soft welcoming flesh under her nightdress. It was a tantalising sensation. He was surprised when she instinctively undid the top button allowing him to kiss her neck. Her mind had raced back to the night at The Crown and Cushion. *He was so dashing, rescuing me like that.* She felt safe with him. Then, with a smile, she remembered how he complimented her at The Ritz, and with that, the last of her resolve evaporated.

David was the sweetest lover, treating Suzanna with the utmost tenderness. He studied her face as he undressed her, sensitive to any sound or expression which could indicate that she was afraid or uncomfortable. He loved her dark skin that contrasted with his as their limbs entwined. Her dark hair that tumbled down her back like the mane of a wild horse.

With the utmost care, he covered her with his body. He did not have to ask her if she wanted to make love—he could feel it in her response to him. Suzanna was the enjoying exquisite pleasure of her first time with a man she cared deeply for. He wanted the moment to be special for her—unforgettable even.   The slight awkwardness she felt from her inexperience was nothing in comparison to the ecstasy that engulfed her. Afterwards, they lay in one another's arms not uttering a word, content to listen to each others soft breathing. David did not tell her that he loved her, and Suzanna did not ask.

Early the next morning, David knew the workers at The Songbird would be taking up their positions and time was of the essence if they were to get back undetected. David washed and dressed for work, then he smuggled Suzanna back to her room, dressing her in one of his big coats and a wide-brimmed hat to hide her long hair.

Her bedroom still had the Parisienne backdrop in situ. He stepped into the French capital for a moment and kissed her again, chastising himself for falling in love with the beautiful exotic creature who he would lose forever at the gala night contest.

13

THE CASUALTY EMERGES

Thomas opened his bedroom door and limped toward the staircase. Unsure if he was suffering a severe concussion when he swore he saw two white bunny rabbits bouncing on the steps watching him from the shadows and thought he might be. Other than hallucinating and a few painful wounds on his torso, he decided he would be right as rain soon.

On the landing, he bumped into Sid.

"Good morning, soldier," Sergeant Payne greeted cheerfully.

"Good morning, Sir," Thomas replied, thinking nothing of indulging Sid's desire to reference his military past.

"Are you aware of the explosion in the early hours of the morning?"

"Yes, Sir. The racket was unmissable," replied Thomas.

"At least, Max and I were able to contain the uprising," confirmed Payne.

He looked at the Sergeant, raising his eyebrows at the curious comment. Thomas, like Max, was spotting the clues that Sergeant Payne seemed to think he was still on a tour of active duty. If the aide were honest, it worried him a little. He'd read in the papers that ex-military men were prone flashbacks and snapping at the slightest bit of provocation. Thomas hoped Payne was not losing his grip on reality.

"It was an attack on our soil," added Sid.

"Quite," Thomas replied, deciding to humour the man.

Well, Payne is certainly in the right environment to have a vivid imagination and curious habits. He will fit in perfectly to this madhouse. Thomas left Sid to his warlike delusions and, feeling peckish at last, went in search of food.

Mrs Bowles had been preparing all the meat that she could preserve for the Christmas Day meals. There was smoked ham hanging in the cold store, and sides of beef soaking in hefty buckets of salted water. She was liberally dousing at least a dozen Christmas cakes with brandy, while she gave her assistant orders on how to steam a plum pudding in a muslin rag. Thomas tried to steal a couple of mince pies cooling on the rack, but Mrs

Bowles caught him. She rapped his knuckles with her ladle then shooed him away. Thomas winced in pain and loosened his grip on the sweet treats. *Please, no more injuries, I've suffered enough.*

Seeing his miserable expression, Mrs Bowles took pity on him.

"You can have one—just one—mind."

Thomas grinned at the news. His arm shot out quicker than a frog's tongue latching onto a fly as he whipped away one of the delectable pies.

"Now, get out from under my feet, Mr Bartlett. Got a to-do list as long as your arm, I have. Max keeps adding to the bloomin' thing. I think when I die, I'll come back as a miracle worker—it'll be a nice rest!"

Thomas winked at Mrs Bowles then scuttled off to the big table and munched on the glorious snack.

*

While the backstage staff at The Songbird worked tirelessly to prepare for the yuletide festivities, it was time for Max and the others to take a break and head off to Lord Ashwood's country estate to hunt the game birds destined for the gala night's formal dinner.

Thomas did not know what he was more excited about, a luxury weekend retreated or pointing a real gun at a clueless bird and shooting the stuffing out of it. As a young lad, at the coast, he enjoyed fishing for crabs at the quayside. Alas, Thomas, a city boy at heart did not have much of an idea about what was involved to put meat on the table. He could not ask Max or David for advice as he was sure they were as inexperienced as he was. *Perhaps Sergeant Payne might pass on a few tips to us.* Then, Thomas began to imagine the chaos that would ensue at the Ashwood Estate if Sergeant Payne went on the rampage with a loaded gun. He decided did not want to find out what that might entail.

Max was adamant Suzanna should accompany them saying he needed his secretary wherever he went. However, Thomas knew that Max loved Suzanna like a daughter, and it was far more likely he wanted her to experience the finery that Lord Ashwood's sumptuous lifestyle had to offer, rather than call upon her administrative assistance.

Ashwood was still smitten with his fiancée, Monique, so everyone presumed she would be there too. Thomas wondered when Peter would begin to see the horrible harridan for what she was, but perhaps that was what rich men wanted—a snooty wife who would fit in with other haughty wives.

Thomas realised how lucky he was as well as everyone else involved with The Songbird's productions. They were all immersed in a world of delight and fantasy, unaffected by class. The artistic license to ply their trade meant they were not subject to societal norms. In the big melting pot that was the auditorium, the rich had their gala nights, posh stalls and boxes and the rest had the regular nights and the cheap seats. *Artists seem to face no judgement, else except in the newspapers, perhaps.* Even then, the critics were only really interested in seeing performances in the comfort of the front row and schmoozing with the stars at the lavish after show parties. Bad reviews were soon forgotten by the paying public when word of mouth would spread wider and longer than a scathing one-off piece in the press.

Thomas was still pondering the benefits of his career when a tall, sad-looking man in a black suit came into the kitchen and slumped down on the chair beside him. The man looked like something between a tax collector and an undertaker. Mrs Bowles made no attempt to chase the man off. He made no effort to greet anybody working at the table or introduce himself, yet he did thank the cook for the meal.

"Who's the grim reaper?" Thomas asked Mrs Bowles after the man had left.

"The new magician," she answered, "I don't know his name yet."

Thomas' mood seemed to lighten instantly. *That must be where those two bunnies came from! Thank goodness! I'm not concussed after all.*

*

Suzanna's mind was focused on the Christmas gala event and the life-changing contest. The date was rapidly approaching.

"Ma, I want to wear a black dress for the competition. Have you got anything that you can alter?" Suzanna had asked Maria.

"What's come over you, Suzanna? Black is for mourning widows and funerals. A bright colour is what you need. I have been ordered to create something spectacular for Monique. We're planning an elegant but daring scarlet gown. Max has said she can choose the most breath-taking earrings from the Liebowitz family collection."

Suzanna rolled her eyes, hardly impressed by her mother's safe and staid plans for her. *I am not a poor man's Monique!* The young girl wanted to make a bold impression, not look like every other singer on the variety circuit.

"I can't see how looking bereaved will endear you to the judges, Suzanna," Maria snapped, irritated by her daughter's desire to be an iconoclast. "How about some brightly coloured ribbons and beads at least?"

"Yes to black. No to the colourful trimmings."

Maria shook her head.

"I am sure that it will be perfect when you have finished it," the girl said with a smile.

"Monique is going to steal the show with the red dress, Suzanna. Is that what you want?"

"That is what she is paid to do, Ma, be the diva, the starlet. Max is just being kind to me. He could easily have chosen someone else to sing—girls would be biting his hand off at the chance. I have no desire to be a prima donna. It is enough reward that I am trusted to be his secretary, let alone participate in such a prestigious competition. Winning is of no consequence."

Maria's face was one of total concentration as her daughter put on the black dress she had slaved over. The seamstress was adamant it would not resemble a mourning garment and applied her creative license to design a simple yet breath-taking gown that would still meet her daughter's approval. With its drop-waisted design and snug bodice, the dress elongated the wearer's torso, enabling Suzanna to reveal her shapely body in a subtle way. The sleeves were off the shoulder, exposing her dark and exotic skin. The skirt velvet had a gossamer-thin layer of soft tulle fabric on the outside. Dotted on the tulle were tiny black beads. The mother knew when her daughter stood under the spotlight, the beads would sparkle with each footstep. The hemline just touched the floor as Suzanna moved, creating the impression that she was gliding gracefully like an angel, not walking.

To complete the ensemble, she insisted that Suzanna wear her hair in an elegant chignon. A simple black ribbon choker with a round diamante pendant sat at her neck, sparkling against her olive skin. Everything inch of Suzanna was elegant, simple and breath-taking.

"I cannot wear this, Mama. I cannot," whispered Suzanna, looking at her reflection, thinking it was a stranger staring back out at her.

"I have not spent a week of late nights making that gown for you to refuse to wear it," Maria growled. "What's wrong with it, pray tell?"

"It is too beautiful. It is more beautiful than I imagined it could be."

"Isn't that the point though? This is a gala competition, Suzanna. I will not allow you to waltz on stage looking like one of those St. Giles women from Sally's."

"It is stunning," Suzanna cooed, swishing the skirt from side to side so she could admire the twinkling beadwork.

"It is," Maria agreed, bursting with pride, "and I am certain you'll be the most beautiful woman in The Songbird on the night."

"Perhaps," came the timid reply as Suzanna got changed into her usual clothes.

Maria shook her head when the girl left. So often she wanted to give her daughter a good shake for her lack of confidence, but somehow managed to stifle the urge.

"Can I come in?" shouted a voice from the doorway.

"Of course, Max. Why I have not seen you for days! I've been trapped in here behind this wretched sewing machine. What have you been up to?"

"Mmmm!" he sighed, "I have been having a few adventures. Have you met Sundatara the elephant yet?"

"No," Maria chuckled, "but I have heard Thomas complaining that thanks to her, our Christmas trees are disappearing at a great rate of knots."

"Well, she is a big hungry girl," laughed Max, "and I have to keep her happy. She is a temperamental thing at times, bless her. It can't be easy settling into a city when she's used to roaming the jungle. It will be worth the trouble though. The crowd will love her—I can feel it in my bones."

"I think it's a fine idea, Max. What could possibly go wrong?" Maria jested, remembering the chaos of Christmases gone by. "You've certainly got a lot of nerve at your age."

"Now, now, Maria! I don't know how to take that comment," Max protested.

He wandered over and sat down in a comfortable chair next to Maria's sewing machine. Over the years, regularly they confided in each other in their hour of need. Whether Max was looking for a voice of reason to assess his latest scheme or a loyal friend to confess to when his confidence was shaken, he would visit Maria and pour his heart out. The lifelong bond was forged because the two of them had similar backgrounds. Both had started from nothing in life and worked their way up. Max Leibowitz, the Polish immigrant had become the director of one of the finest theatres in London. Maria, the unwed mother was now head seamstress and costume designer at The Songbird. As single parents, they had been forced to raise their children without a spouse, and many a night they had sought advice from each other about their offspring.

"I would love Suzanna to win the competition, Maria. It would do her confidence the power of good. After honing her craft in Florence she would be the talk of London on her return. This theatre needs a true songbird. Right now we have a blasted 'song vulture'."

"Now, Max. Don't be ungrateful. Monique ensures the theatre is full night after night. You can't complain."

"I thought that too," he replied, "—until I watched Suzanna. I've seen enough acts in my time to know that she has true star potential, even if she might not think so."

"Yes, she sang beautifully. I was so proud of her the last time she appeared here. She just needs a little more confidence and she will soar to success."

"And she is such a gentle soul, Maria. These days, Monique is spiteful and begrudging. I am tiring of her petulance. These days, I thank the Lord I am retiring. Then she will become Thomas or David's problem. I don't know what Lord Ashwood sees in that harpy at times. She can't love him, she only loves herself!"

Maria allowed Max to vent but did not divulge her opinion on Monique. She had been brought up not to say something behind someone's back that should not be said to their face.

"Max, I know that Suzanna has enough talent to win this competition, but I am afraid for her."

"How so?" asked Max. "She'll get over the stage fright once she's a couple of songs into her act. They all do."

"No. It's not that. You'll remember I've told you about Suzanna's Gypsy father—"

It was precisely at that moment that Monique opened the door without knocking first. She looked at Maria, and then at Max, then turned and stared at Maria again.

"Can I help you?" Maria demanded impatiently.

"Excusez-moi! I didn't know that you and Max were having a tête-à-tête. I will come back," said Monique, as a small smile appeared on her lips.

Unable to contain her joy, the diva left the room and danced down the stairs in delight and relief.

"Do you think she heard what I said?" asked a worried-looking Maria.

"I hope not," Max replied gravely.

"If the news of her parentage reaches the social columns in the newspaper, they will make Suzanna's life a misery. The Roma community have been portrayed in such a terrible light in the press as scoundrels. She has been happy and safe here. You took us under your wing and protected us for years. I don't want this ugly business surfacing— especially now with the contest of her dreams in her sights!"

"Try not to worry, Maria, my dear. I'll never let anyone hurt Suzanna."

"But Max," the concerned mother protested, "you know being a Gypsy is worse than being a dog! Not only in England but all over Europe. Her chances in Italy are doomed before they even started. What was I doing when I went with Ocean Taylor all those years ago? The stigma will plague my child forever!"

Max took her hand and held it gently.

"If you hadn't met that Gypsy fellow, you would never have had Suzanna, and all our lives would be the poorer for it. Some good came out of the encounter. Cling onto that thought."

Tears of dread began to form in Maria's eyes. *I've hidden my family secret for years, and now, in a moment of rashness, the most spiteful, selfish and vindictive woman in London knows.* Max sensed her angst and tried to reassure her.

"Maria, it will damage Suzanna far more if we teach her to be ashamed of herself. She is a fine, beautiful woman who emanates kindness and joy wherever she goes. Remind me—she does she know who her father is?"

"Yes. I felt it was wrong to keep it from her— or tell her little white lies. But if this becomes public information, they will persecute her. Monique is bound to use it as a weapon if it furthers her own interests."

"I don't know what makes people hate someone different from them, Maria. It makes no sense."

"Ocean told me that our Queen sold his people as slaves, that they were put to death without fair trials. The 'lucky ones' were whipped and tortured in public. All the while the newspapers published them to be thieves and murderers. There's no wonder the public harbour such a grudge. They were painted in such a terrible light. And the stories from the continent are no better. There has prejudice there too— for centuries."

Max nodded slowly, listening to Maria, understanding first-hand what persecution feels like.

"Ever since the Romany people arrived in Europe in the 1400s, they endured expulsions. Their children were forcibly taken from them. The was compulsory servitude in galleys or mines. Every Gypsy in the Balkans was marked as a slave. It's all bubbling under the surface of polite society in Europe. Even if she won the competition and escaped the prejudice in England, there would be no respite in Italy."

"I can see why you are fearful, my dear. I am your friend, Maria, and we have walked a long road together. You can rely on my support."

Maria gave Max a sad smile. He decided to lighten the mood.

"Is that how you look when your child is about to become the most famous singer in England and Europe? You, the mother of the legendary Songbird Theatre's new star?" he teased.

Maria giggled silently. Max always made her feel better. He was the eternal optimist giving everybody around him endless hope, no matter how dark their situation.

"Let's see what happens on Saturday night, Max. I know that Suzanna will do her best."

14

THE THREAT OF THE CHALLENGER

Suzanna's performance of Habanera was still haunting Monique. As late as the afternoon before the competition, she was still plotting how she could dissuade Suzanna from participating, or better still engineer her nemesis' downfall. *Losing the Gypsy girl from the contest will make my chance to audition in Florence a dead cert.*

Monique had guessed correctly that David Liebowitz was in love with Suzanna. Although David was a more loyal man than Peter Ashwood, and she was sure he would not take kindly to learning of Suzanna's wayward Gypsy blood and his father's decades of deceit.

Monique also had plans to use David to further her own ends. She knew he was a handsome man—blond hair, blue-eyed and a body fit for a warrior. She allowed her mind to wander further. The idea of seducing David had endless appeal. *Bedding him would be an excellent shortcut to progressing my career.* She imagined how life would be if she married David. *I'll be the true queen of The Songbird.* Oh, how she would entertain! Then she imagined raising the status of the theatre further still by courting the upper class with luxury gala evenings. *The days of letting in all and sundry for a cheap night's entertainment will be over.*

Monique was shocked into the present by the racket the rowdy ladies from Sally's were making in the next room. *What was Max thinking when he allowed that sort of woman to move in? How can he drop his standards so low? It won't be long before those unholy cows begin enticing patrons into their makeshift boudoir. I will be performing in a den of iniquity—not a theatre!*

*

Max sat opposite David who was dressed in a perfectly tailored suit and looking well-turned-out, as ever.

"About Suzanna," Max began the conversation.

David looked up from a pile of books that he was reading.

"What about Suzanna?" he asked.

"You could not have chosen a more beautiful person to love, David. I have always held that girl dear in my heart."

David kept quiet, and let his gaze fall back to the book, hoping that Max would change the subject.

"Have you asked her to marry you yet?"

"No, Papa," he sighed.

Max rolled his eyes to the heavens.

"Why is it so important that I marry?" asked David with irritation.

"I want grandchildren. I want a family again."

"Look around, Papa," chided David. "This place is full of children. Every time I take a walk, I see at least two whom I have never seen before. Even Mrs Bowles has her grandchildren running around here for the holidays."

"Are you trying to tell me that you will never give me grandchildren?" demanded Max heatedly.

"You cannot order children like you order potatoes," countered David.

"Suzanna is a young and healthy lass," said Max lifting a bushy grey eyebrow provocatively.

David ignored him.

"You don't look very happy for a man in love," Max laughed loudly.

"Forget about Suzanna, Papa. It's not meant to be."

"Why do you say that? What has happened? You've not had a tiff already, have you?"

"Of course not. It's quite simple. If Suzanna wins your stupid singing contest, she will go to Florence, join their opera, and I will never see her again. I have been foolish to allow myself close to her. It will only end in heartache for us both. That's why I've decided to cool things off."

Max nodded his head, realising his son had a point. He felt a pang of guilt for giving David's sweetheart a place in the competition. *Did I do the right thing?*

"What did Suzanna say about the audition? Does she even want to go? It's a big step. She might just want the chance to perform at the Gala night. It's not set in stone that she will go to Italy if she wins."

"But it is, Papa. Suzanna says Florence will be a dream come true. I can't stop her. I won't stop her. She will resent me for the rest of my life," David said mournfully.

"You are right, son," agreed Max, "you can't hold her back."

"Remind me, when does the winner leave for Italy?" asked David.

"Immediately after the concert. Puccini is premiering Tosca in the middle of January, and she will get a small part in that, I expect. It's a very tight deadline."

"I am beginning to hate Christmas."

"Don't say that, David! Christmas is a time of exceptional joy," Max chastised.

"Papa, there is another option, I suppose?" said David, seriously. "What would happen if I don't take over The Songbird when you retire?"

"That is a strange question, my son. You know making the place a success has been my life's work. I always assumed—"

David cut him off.

"—I have come to realise that I have lived in this place all my life, surrounded by hordes of people and suffocated with mountains of work. I want a simpler existence. And one day when I marry for love, I want a homely, quiet place where I can spend time with my wife and those grandchildren that you continually insist upon."

"David, I have built this business from nothing—put my heart and soul into it," Max reiterated. "I can see you are unhappy here. I can see it every time I walk into this office. Much as my dream might be for you to take over, I feel the same as you feel about Suzanna, I can't hold you back either if your future lies elsewhere."

"Will you sell The Songbird?"

"I don't think it will come to that. Besides, it's my pension. In fact, it's a lucrative business that will support us all well."

David raised his eyebrows. *It could support us a damn side better if you stopped housing all these 'people in need'. Or hungry elephants.*

"No, I will not sell it. I'll give young Thomas first refusal on co-owning it with me. I am sure he could secure some funding."

"Are you sure?"

"Of course! Thomas loves this theatre, and he knows everything about it. He loves the people and the drama. With him as the new full-time manager, it will also allow me to come and visit regularly," Max added with a laugh.

"I thought you would be furious with me, Papa," said David with relief.

"Not at all, son. Living another man's dream is a nightmare."

15

GALA NIGHT ARRIVES

On the night of the gala, a great excitement gripped The Songbird. It was destined to be the evening that everyone would remember. The enthusiasm was contagious, as if the audience was aware that something extraordinary was going to happen. Everybody behind the scenes was a bag of nerves. Several of them had secretly taken a sneaky peek at the patrons as they assembled, trying to guess which person was representing the Florence opera.

Max stood in the shadows, watching the people arriving, looking refined in his white dinner jacket and matching white bow tie. Thomas was wearing a dress suit which was unusual for the young aide who was more often seen in some scruffy looking overalls and giving orders in the wings all night.

David had placed himself on the mezzanine level, high above the stage. He was never eager to get swamped by the crowd. He wore a perfectly pressed black dinner suit. Nobody would deny that David was a handsome man. His ash-blond hair was cut in a severe style, enhancing his air of sophistication and making his startling blue eyes and strong jaw the focus of attention.

Max sent a young stagehand up the steel staircase to tell David the Italian ambassador and his entourage were due to arrive and that his attendance was mandatory. He made for the front steps of the theatre and proudly stood next to his father. Four carriages of dignitaries arrived. There was no mistaking the Italians with their tanned skins and glamourous slick black hair. David remembered Italian men were supposed to love blonde women and wondered if that would count in Monique's favour. *Mind you, the Italians are not particularly fond of the French after half a century of hostility, so perhaps that will count for nothing.*

The Italian women were some of the most fashionable and elegant that David had ever encountered. They dressed so impeccably they made even the most stylish British woman look like a frump. *I wonder if Suzanna will begin dressing like an Italian if she goes to Florence? How many more times—I need to forget about her.* Jewellery was in abundance, from bold gold rings for the men to diamonds and rubies for their wives, tastefully applied, yet enough to outshine the demure English. They persisted with their continental style of greeting, making a show of politely kissing each cheek. The handsome young Brit experienced each hot-blooded belladonna push her body up close to his and linger a few seconds too long.

Thomas enjoyed every moment of the introduction, making the most of greeting Francesco de Renzis' divine daughters. They fluttered their beautiful lush eyelashes at him unashamedly and introduced themselves by their first names.

Monique and Suzanna were not in the welcoming party. Max was afraid that it would cause bias. Both women were still in their dressing rooms, suffering pre-show anxiety. Both were holding court with their supporters.

An elite group of Peter Ashwood's friends were drinking champagne with the French diva. Her dressing room was a picture of sophistication, fit for royalty. A simmering Ashwood stood on the peripheries of the small crowd watching Monique lap up adoration like a thirsty dog would a bowl of water. The scene began to disgust him. *She side-lines me whenever someone 'better' comes along.* Her arrogance, feeling she could get away with treating him so shabbily in public and that he would still come running like a soppy little puppy was becoming unbearable.

Suzanna's dressing room could not have been more different. Chaos rather than sophistication reigned supreme. She was surrounded by Sally's girls who were drinking cheap gin out of pint glasses and offering their advice while Maria dressed her. The rowdy lasses had some outlandish suggestions, and Suzanna laughed so much she was afraid that her daughter would split the sides of her tight bodice.

The proud mother was grateful for the cheery atmosphere. It took Maria's mind off Monique De La Marre knowing the truth about Suzanna's Gypsy father. As yet, the diva seemed to have kept the revelation to herself, and Maria was tempted to think perhaps Monique hadn't overheard the tail end of her conversation with Max after all. She was wrong.

The audience rose to their feet and gently applauded when the Italian contingent were shown to their seats. Ambassador Francesco de Renzis made an opening speech hailing opera singers as more spectacular than royalty—'one step away from gods' he said at one point. David was sure that the pope would have burnt him at the stake if he had heard the speech.

He excused himself, went backstage and waited for Suzanna to arrive. Monique appeared first with her sycophantic friends. Her bright red sequined dress showed as much soft white flesh as she could muster without causing too much offence. Her hair was styled to show off her blonde tresses, in the hope that it would seduce the red-blooded male judges.

David greeted Peter Ashwood with a handshake.

"May the best woman win," Peter quipped. "I wish you all the best."

"Thank you, and to you as well. I will pass the message to Suzanna."

David smiled, but he could not share Ashcroft's enthusiasm. *Suzanna is the best woman, and when she wins, I will have lost her—forever.*

Suzanna floated toward David. The timid little girl he raced around the theatre with as a child was now a sophisticated performer ready to face the crowd. As she walked towards him, in her mind, David was the only person in the room. As she reached him, she gazed into his eyes passionately. He held out his arms to her. She allowed him to kiss her on the cheek, mimicking the Italians earlier. Ashwood watched them from where he stood and his jealousy flared up. *Why can't I find a beautiful woman who would look at me like she looks at David? Monique barely acknowledges me these days.*

Monique was going to sing first. She walked onto the stage and blew a kiss to her supporters in the wings. With her head held high, she stood behind the luxurious red velvet curtain, waiting for it to open slowly.

The curtains parted. The audience stood up and applauded Monique, who smiled and dropped her head in acknowledgement of their adoration. She expected nothing less than total devotion from them and was delighted to receive it on such an important night in her career. *Magnifique! The judges will see how much this British audience loves me! And so it will be in Italy!*

Monique chose to sing an aria by the Italian composer, Puccini's, 'Musetta's Waltz' from La Bohème. She could not have chosen a better song to sum up her personality.

When I walk all alone in the street,
people stop and stare at me
and look for my whole beauty
from head to feet...

Deliberately choosing an aria with Italian lyrics, the entire piece was a musical projection of Monique's narcissism. She was a gifted woman who entranced the audience with her powerful timbre and vocal range. Performing with such serene confidence and natural talent, she was sure that the judges would choose her. Backstage, she had already packed her luggage in eager anticipation of her imminent journey to Florence. With all her heart she believed it was time to bid farewell to miserable, boring, London.

Monique paraded about the stage, going through the motions of her routine that she had performed thousands of times already, delivering her songs with conviction and passion. The whole performance was polished and professional.

Most of Monique's set had been operatic, but it ended with a change of tempo as she belted out the music hall staple, 'The Man on the Flying Trapeze'. The audience gleefully clapped along, singing their hearts out to the popular tune. The rafters were definitely being raised. It looked and sounded like the crowd were eating out of Monique's hand as she entertained them. Her set ended with rapturous applause.

"Don't be afraid, Suzanna," David said gently, as the curtain fell on Monique's act.

With everyone backstage still transfixed by the starlet's magical performance, Suzanna gave David a grateful peck on the cheek for his kind words, then held her mouth close to his ear.

"There is nothing for me to fear. I will have your beautiful face right in front of me," she whispered.

As she turned to walk on the stage, Suzanna's back was straight, and her chin was up. Her posture was magnificent, and her genuine warm smile charmed her way into the Italians' hearts from the moment they saw her. She floated into the spotlight, with the beads on her dress twinkling at the audience. The Italian women were impressed with the bold statement made by her black outfit. It was as innovative as anything that they could buy in Milan. The men were captivated by her dark exotic beauty, her skin tone looking sunkissed and healthy, despite it being the middle of the harsh British winter.

The audience held their breath in anticipation to hear Suzanna sing. She had been the talk of theatreland after her last performance at The Songbird, and soon they would hear the fresh-faced newcomer once again.

Conductor Hoffman lifted his baton, and the orchestra started to play the introduction to Carmen's Habanera. Suzanna began the song note-perfect and with a blistering confidence that David had never imagined that she could summon.

On stage, she transformed herself into a Spanish Gypsy. Her inhibitions fell away. She was lost in the music and lived through the song. Her body and soul portrayed Carmen searching for love. Impressed by her deep connection to the music, the audience could tell she wasn't just singing the lyrics, she was living them before their very eyes.

At the end of her first song, the audience was enraptured. Their delight in her soared higher still by the end of her set, feeding off her enthusiasm as she sang. As the orchestra played the last few bars, a humble and grateful Suzanna curtsied to the crowd, her face light up with true joy. Compared with Monique and her peacocking, Suzanna's humility was touching.

Stunning bouquets of flowers thrown by Suzanna's supporters landed at the front of the wooden stage and skidded towards her feet. The crowd were chanting for more, and since she was the second artiste on the billing, Suzanna seized the opportunity to continue. *I must prove to Max I can replace Monique when she leaves The Songbird.*

She gave Conductor Hoffman a cheeky wink. Hoffman was delighted to get an opportunity to infuriate the diva, and with a swift flick of his baton, the orchestra sprang into life once more with the opening notes of Suzanna's strongest song, Marie Lloyd's signature tune, 'The Boy I Love Is Up in the Gallery'. She forgot about the horrors of The Crown and Cushion and imagined David's face as she closed her eyes and immersed herself in the tune, loving every second of the attention.

The boy I love is up in the gallery
The boy I love is looking now at me
There he is, can't you see, waving his
handkerchief
As merry as a robin that sings on a tree

Monique stood off stage, surrounded by her shallow friends. Alas, they were ignoring her, all of them as taken with Suzanne as everyone else in the auditorium. The diva did her best to remain the image of decorum and grace, but in the end, she failed miserably. On the verge of tears, she ran to her dressing room, mortified. Alone, a distraught Monique sobbed into a cushion on her chaise longue. Her dramatic stage make-up dribbled from her lashes and down her pale cheeks in long black streams. For the first time in her professional life, Monique had to consider she might not have the upper hand.

Back on stage, Suzanna was winding up her encore with a lively rendition of 'Where did you get that hat.' The audience's happy voices ringing out and filling the theatre with joy. It made Monique feel worse. *She has the crowd eating out of her hand.*

There was a gentle knock on the door. The diva grabbed a tissue and desperately scrubbed at her face. The reflection in the mirror shocked her. She looked weak and disconsolate—nothing like her stage persona at all. There was another knock at the door, much louder this time. With nowhere to hide, Monique summoned up the courage to open it. It was Max, stood outside, looking relaxed with his hands in his pockets. The empathy on his face was plain to see. She threw her arms around his neck, hid her face in the curve of his neck and began to sob uncontrollably.

"What are all these tears for, my dear? You sang beautifully. The audience was enthralled as ever," Max said encouragingly, trying desperately to calm her.

"Yes, but they loved her. They didn't love me," she protested between snatched uncontrollable breaths.

With no further words of comfort, Max held her until she stopped trembling, stroking her hair reassuringly. Besides, he agreed with the diva. It was obvious there had been a special rapport between Susanna and the audience during her spirited act that had been missing from Monique's perfect, but clinical, performance.

"Susanna only has one song left. Then the judges will be ready to announce the winner, Monique. You must be there."

"I can't face anybody. Tell them that I am indisposed. Tell the ambassador that I am ill," she wailed, thinking only of herself as usual.

Max was livid. *How dare she snub the audience and the ambassador's entourage like that! And me! Who does she think she is? I am tired of her tantrums.*

"Wash your face and stop crying at once. You are a professional. Start behaving like one," he said firmly. "If you choose to defy me, I will send somebody to carry you down. How dare you consider embarrassing me in front of these important people—people who have been willing to offer you an opportunity of a lifetime?"

Monique knew not to argue with Max. She had never seen him this furious. Filled with terror, she obeyed him. In a frosty silence, the two of them stomped back towards the wings. He snapped his fingers and gestured for two young stylists to attend to Monique's appearance. They quickly set to work, and the diva was quickly transformed to her usual beauty.

To demonstrate her versatility, Suzanna finished her encore with an Italian aria of her own, 'O mio babbino caro' from Puccini's 'Gianni Schicchi'. She ended the performance with a gracious bow, then picked up the biggest bunch of flowers by her feet and hugged the blooms close to her chest to show her gratitude. All on their feet, the ecstatic crowd waved and cheered wildly.

David watched Suzanna turn to leave the stage, both of them bursting with pride at her performance. She hid with him in the wings, desperate to share a moment alone with him.

"I am so proud of you," he congratulated. "You did marvellously! You even had a standing ovation."

"Are you taking your favourite singer to The Ritz again?" she laughed.

"Yes, I am."

"Thank you for believing in me, David. It means everything. Without you by my side, I wouldn't have even had the courage to compete."

Hidden in the shadows, he looked into her eyes, totally transfixed by her, doing his best to ignore their imminent separation, the thought of which was cutting through his heart like a knife.

"It was my pleasure! Like my father, I will always support you," he blurted out, hoping his voice would not waver with emotion.

"Once Monique is announced the winner, can we leave? I can't face watching her strut about rubbing my nose into her victory."

He leaned forward, desperate to kiss her, to celebrate her success and to say farewell, but it was not to be.

"Suzanna!" yelled Thomas. "Where the devil are you?"

"Over here!" she confirmed as she pulled away from David.

"Come on, then! The judges are calling for you and Monique."

Monique put her best foot forward and breezed past Susanna, and onto the stage to a loud cheer. Suzanna looked back at her beau, knowing she had to go, but not wanting to say goodbye just yet. She walked away, giving him an alluring smile over her shoulder. He beamed back at her but ached inside. *Tonight, she will be gone, I know it.*

The two rival women stood alongside each other at the left of the stage. The ambassador and his wife were at the right, standing behind the podium normally reserved for the compere. Francesco looked at the notes he had prepared, then cleared his throat.

"Ladies and gentlemen," the ambassador began, "it gives me great pleasure to announce the winner of this prize. It has been a very difficult decision. The award goes to an exceptional lady."

Always wanting to put on a show, Monique smiled confidently, despite her earlier concerns.

"This prize will enable the winner to audition for the prestigious Florence School of Opera."

David wished Francesco would stop blathering on and get on with it. *Will I lose her?*

"And the winner is—"

The audience gasped. The ambassador stalled for dramatic effect.

"—Miss Suzanne Stratton. Congratulations. Tonight, we depart to Florence!"

Savouring the underdog's triumph, the crowd got to their feet, delighted that the fresh-faced English rose had defeated the haughty established French starlet. Suzanna felt dazed. The noise of another standing ovation was overwhelming. The large spotlight blinded her and swathes of people that she did not know were coming to congratulate her. There were more continental kisses from the Italians.

David fought his way through the people and reached her side. She heard his voice and turned to face it. He took her in his arms and hugged Suzanna to his chest, and then he quickly kissed her on the cheek.

"You are lovely," he whispered in her ear, "I am so proud of you."

David was emotional. *This is it. She really is going.* Had he been alone, he sensed he would have cried. With his throat tightened by anguish and his stomach in knots, he let his arms fall away from her. It was then that she panicked.

"Don't leave me, David. Stay next to me. I don't want to be alone. I am not used to all of this attention."

He looked down at her, his red stinging eyes threatening to well up. He did not want to let her go, but he had no choice. She had won and would be leaving him for Italy as planned.

"Susannah!" Max shouted over the congratulatory cacophony. "Thomas has brought your trunk down from your room. It's time to get to the station. The ambassador's valet will help you. You don't want to miss tonight's sailing to France, my girl, do you?"

"Please come with me, David? Please?"

Blinking furiously, trying to squash away his tears, he nodded.

*

All too soon it was time for the farewell at the platform.

"Send me a telegram when you reach Florence. Tell me how wonderful it all is?"

"I will."

"And write to me occasionally and tell me how your lessons are going? Perhaps I can visit you in the summertime?"

"Yes, I would like that. Enjoy the Christmas show. Max will be—"

A loud train whistle interrupted her. The stagehands lugged her trunk onto the train. Suzanna felt herself choking up as the moment to leave was upon them. Talking became difficult. David put his arms around her, then kissed her in full view of everyone. Some passengers turned away in shock, others smirked.

"I will bring you home if you're unhappy, Suzanna."

She nodded at him. He put his arms around her again, fighting back the words he had to tell her before she left. Feeling her warm breath against his neck, he gave in.

"I love you, Suzanna."

"I love you too, David. I wish you could come with me. The summer seems a lifetime away."

"Time will fly. And we can write. Go now. There is a great adventure ahead of you."

David watched her get into the carriage and take a seat with the Ambassador and his wife. The trio struck up a friendly-looking conversation immediately. He waved at her, but she wasn't looking, too engrossed with entertaining her travelling companions. He had seen her almost every day for twenty-two-years, but it was over. She really was all grown up, and it was time for her to follow her dreams.

The heartbroken young man watched the train puff and pant its way out of London Bridge station and disappear into the black of night.

16

THE FROSTY WALK IN THE WOODS

A few days later, deciding to transport his guests the short distance to his country manor in style, Lord Ashwood booked two private train compartments.

Monique arrived at London Paddington dressed in a luxurious fur coat that covered her from head to foot, looking regal. When a platform attendant stepped aside to let her pass, Monique behaved like a medieval monarch, staring down her nose at the peasants in her way. Showing no decency, no one was thanked if they made way for her. She was followed by a porter who had the unfortunate task of taking care of three trunks of clothing and four hat boxes that were accompanying her for the short weekend break. Thomas couldn't believe that one person could need that many clothes. *I could fit everything I own into one trunk—the posh clothes and the tatty ones.*

When it was time to board, the guard sought out Monique and escorted her to a first-class cabin. Lord Ashwood had afforded his friend Max that courtesy. Besides, the diva would have chewed his ears for doing anything less. The rest of the party had to squeeze into the other compartment, luggage and all. To make matters worse, Max had invited Sergeant Payne for the weekend, assuring Lord Ashwood that the man's military experience would be of great benefit to those who had never hunted.

In the second-class carriage, five people were squashed into a space made for four. Madeleine, Monique's svelte overworked maid, wedged herself in between the two slender men, David and Thomas, opposite portly Max and the immense bulk of Sergeant Payne. Sid told them old war stories as the train rumbled along, believing that he was alleviating the boredom.

"Why is your voice so rasping, Sergeant?"
asked young Madeleine, during a brief pause
in the monologue.

Max's eyes widened. He quickly nipped the situation in the bud, relieved that Payne, back full flow, appeared not to hear.

"Terrible accident, my dear, terrible accident."

"Oh my," gasped Madeleine. "Perhaps he can
tell us the story?" she whispered.

Max's eyes became wider still. He glared at the girl and shook his head vehemently. Thankfully for Max, she obeyed her boss and did not say a word for the rest of the journey.

Bored with the war stories, David's gaze drifted onto the passing countryside. He thought of his sweetheart, remembering the heart wrenching night of her departure. *I wish that Thomas had never suggested that blasted competition. Why had Papa not arranged a raffle or an auction or something equally ridiculous? If he had not been insistent on getting his way yet again—Suzanna would still be with me.*

As the train puffed into the platform at its final destination, a tiny rural station in the middle of nowhere, Lord Ashwood and valet were eagerly awaiting the guests. It was bitingly cold and the winter sky was dismal and grey. The trees, bare of leaves, made the frosty landscape seem a stark black and white.

Peter welcomed them all with a firm handshake as his entourage of servants appeared and began transferring their luggage to the cabs. Again, there were two coaches to transport everyone, but this time Max was invited to travel with Lord Ashwood and Monique and Madeleine. The diva had not spoken a word to max since the night of the contest, and she was thinking of how she would manipulate the situation in her favour.

"My word, Peter, you certainly live in a beautiful part of the world," Max praised.

"It is nothing compared to the landscape around my parents' chateau," interrupted

Monique boastfully. "That has been in our family for two hundred years."

"Yes, of course, dear," Lord Ashwood muttered.

"I could easily live in the country all year round, Max. I don't enjoy the city much. I only go to London to do business."

"And to visit me of course," added Monique.

"Yes, my sweet—and to visit you," Ashwood replied out of habit.

"I could never live in the countryside," complained the singer. "I would be bored to tears, oui? I miss the sophistication of the city."

"When we are married, you may have to reassess your relationship with the city, my dear," Lord Ashwood advised.

"Many couples live apart, oui? Like Sisi and Emperor Franz Josef. I can be in London and you can come and visit me."

Good grief. She's comparing herself to an empress now! Max looked out the window and shook his head gently, reflecting on how unpleasant it was to work with someone with such a strong sense of entitlement. *How can Peter consider living with her for the rest of his life?*

Ashwood's manor was stunning, the epitome of a fine English residence. The lawn was perfectly mowed. Bare winter trees stood on the peripheries of the garden, planted to provide shade on hot summer days. A frozen pond stood in the centre of the courtyard, yet David could imagine barefoot children running around it in the summertime and splashing in the cool water. *I would love a home in the countryside. I long to wake up every morning with my gorgeous wife in my arms and hear the laughter of our children.*

David helped Madeleine out of the coach. The young girl was filled with wonderment when she saw the magnificent manor. She had been in a daydream for days, anticipating the visit to the countryside. Orphaned at a young age, she had never been on a family daytrip out of London, making the exposure to the fresh, wide-open English landscape a genuine novelty to her. Even the fast train ride which everybody else took for granted filled her with awe.

In the coach en route to the manor house, Monique had chastised Madeline for being slow and lacking concentration. Of course, the girl was distracted—she had never been on such an incredible adventure. Madeleine was sure she would have plenty to tell her friends when she returned to The Songbird.

Lord Ashwood's staff were friendly and amenable without being intrusive. Max was relieved to note that Peter seemed a decent employer and his workers cheerful. The aristocracy was renowned for behaving disgracefully towards their servants, but not Ashwood.

He spoke to them kindly and with respect. Max hoped that some of his manners would brush off on Monique as he overheard the starlet talking to young Madeleine.

"You will unpack my trunks, and then you will dismiss yourself and go to the servant's quarters. I do not want to see or hear from you unless I ask for you directly."

"Yes, Miss Monique," replied the girl.

"How many more times, you imbecile. You address me as 'Mademoiselle Monique'," the diva scolded.

As they waited on the gravel driveway, Max discreetly summoned the butler, Jenkins, to his side, took the man's arm and steered him toward Monique and Madeleine. Max addressed the butler in front of the two women.

"Sir, which would be the finest room in the manor?"

"You are the guest of honour, Sir. It will be your room."

"Can I trouble you for a favour, Jenkins?"

"Of course, Sir."

"Please put young Madeleine into my room, and move me to another."

"Yes, Sir," replied the butler, a little baffled by the request. Madeline's startled face looked a picture.

"Oh, and Jenkins, please ensure that there is a place setting for her at every meal."

Monique scowled at Max and the butler, annoyed that Max was happy to override convention to favour the girl.

"Yes, Sir."

"May I ask, what are the features of Madeleine's room?"

"It is a suite, Sir. I mean, Miss. There is a parlour, a bedroom and a water closet."

"That sounds perfect," Max added with a smile that he directed in open-mouthed Madeleine's direction.

To aggravate Monique a little more, Max made further polite requests.

"Please ensure that Madeleine's suite is kept heated. I would like her woken with a cup of tea at seven o'clock every morning and brought a cup of hot chocolate evening before she sleeps. Please turn her bed down by eight o'clock at night. I insist upon a basket of fresh fruit and flowers for her every morning. Pastries are in order in case she wakes up hungry. Please respond to her bell immediately. She is your priority. Afford her all the luxury that you would afford me."

"Right you are, Sir."

Now, Jenkins was as furious as Madeleine's mistress. *Who does that old man think he is? Ordering me to bow and scrape to a woman so inferior? How dare he!*

Eventually, Monique could no longer keep quiet.

"What do you think you are doing, Max? How can you embarrass me like this? She is my maid. If anyone should have the best room in the house, it should be me as Lord Ashcroft's fiancée. That is my room normally."

"I employ Madeleine just as I employ you. She is not your servant. She is your colleague. I am sure your alternative room will be perfectly suitable for your needs, Monique. Peter's home is like a palace. And I am sure, next time you come to stay, you can enjoy the suite, can you not?"

Monique's face flushed with anger. She clenched her jaw and stormed through the grand entrance.

"Take me to my 'new' room," she commanded Jenkins, leaving the others behind to fend for themselves.

When she reached her room she demanded the butler wait outside. She marched to the writing desk and penned a note to Ashwood. She advised Jenkins she was excusing herself for the rest of the day as she felt unwell. As he walked to take the note to his master, she demanded to be served dinner in her bedroom at eight o'clock. He couldn't wait for the harridan to return to London and as far away from his as possible.

"You were joking about swapping rooms, were you, Mr Liebowitz?" asked the awestruck Madeleine.

"No, I was not joking, my dear," Max said kindly. "You have worked tirelessly for all year at Monique's beck and call. Go and enjoy yourself, you've certainly earned a rest! You are my guest of honour for the weekend."

He smiled, then he bent over and whispered in her ear.

"Ring that bell whenever you want something and tell me if they are nasty to you."

Madeleine couldn't believe her luck!

17

NOT THE USUAL
YULETIDE FESTIVITIES

When they stepped inside, it was clear Peter Ashwood always went to great lengths to make his guests feel welcome during the yuletide. Small sprigs of holly tastefully adorned the picture frames. Each of the reception rooms had a perfectly decorated Christmas tree that almost reached the ceiling. Thomas looked around him and nodded in appreciation, stealing some of the creative display ideas to use at The Songbird for next year. There were candles everywhere in tiny silver lanterns strung over the mantlepieces. There was mistletoe above every door frame. Everyone assumed it was a last-ditch attempt by Peter to warm his French fiancée to the festive season and defrost her. The most spectacular of the decorations was a life-size marble sculpture of the nativity scene in the main hallway. Madeleine couldn't begin to imagine how much that might have cost. The small party waited courteously next to it, taking in the grandeur of the place.

"Now, dear friends. You've had a long journey," said Peter. "Go and make yourselves comfortable and settle into your rooms. Let us reconvene at, say, seven o'clock? I'm afraid my fiancée is suffering from one of her headaches and won't be joining us this evening."

No one seemed particularly surprised after her petulant behaviour earlier.

In the early evening, Peter seated his visitors in a cosy parlour off the dining room. Rich oriental carpet covered the floor, and deep red velvet curtains hung at the windows which kept in the heat. They sank back into deep leather chairs, warming their bones in front of a toasty crackling fire. The occasional tables dotted around the room had an array of Christmas treats: delicate mince pies, salt-encrusted pretzels and stollen. Peter wowed his guests when he explained the luxury imported German cake was designed to represent the Christ-child wrapped in swaddling rags. The most sumptuous treat was a silver jug of rich eggnog, made with the thickest cream and richest eggs, carefully ladled into silver goblets by Jenkins' steady hand, each one topped with a light sprinkle of freshly grated nutmeg.

The group sat quietly, taking in the serenity of the moonlit countryside through the parlour's large bay windows. David loved the stillness. There were no teetering piles of ledgers blocking his view. Nobody was knocking on his door interrupting his peace. There was no commotion from artistes practising for the show, nor the clang of pots and pans in the kitchen accompanied by the jabber of women. The parlour was a serene space to simply sit and be. He loved it.

Jenkins rang the ornate golden gong and the party made their way to the dining room. The lavish porcelain tableware had been deployed, along with the baroque-style gold and silver candelabras. The linen was smoother than a fresh sheet of crisp white paper. A seemingly endless array of delectable dishes arrived, served by Jenkins and his highly trained team. Everyone politely ignored the empty chair next that should have been Monique's. The meal was rounded off with port for the Madeleine and cognac for the men.

The guests were all warm and fed, and a drowsy feeling washed over them. One by one, everyone from The Songbird began to excuse themselves and make their way to bed. Jenkins had ensured that gentle fires were dancing brightly in the hearths to make their rooms welcoming and warm, but not hot and stuffy.

Madeleine opened the door to her suite and tip-toed into it, feeling as if she was in a dream. A canopied bed stood in the centre of the room. The floral eiderdown matched the curtains, and there were two blankets underneath it. The Egyptian cotton bedsheets felt luxurious under her hands and she looked forward to sinking her tired head onto a luxuriously fluffy duck-down pillow. Next to her bed was a bunch of beautiful freshly cut blooms. Madeleine could not imagine where they had come from as the ground outside was bare and frozen.

There was a knock on the door, and a maid entered carrying a silver tray with a cup of rich hot chocolate topped with whipped cream and a dusting of cocoa powder. The maid put it down next to a basket of luscious fresh fruit. Again, the young girl wondered where they had found such succulent juicy produce in the middle of winter.

> "They're from Lord Ashcroft's Orangery on the estate, Miss Madeleine. I'll ask Jenkins to show you tomorrow while the men go off to the woods. I'm sure he won't mind."

The young girl had no idea what an Orangery was but looked forward to finding out. She climbed into the warm bed and got lost in the soft fleecy blankets. It was a dream, all a dream, and she was convinced would wake up in the staff quarters at The Songbird in the morning.

*

For the menfolk, the hunt began at noon precisely. Max studied his son carefully as they walked toward the woods. David looked decidedly unhappy. The concerned father had noticed that since Suzanna had left for Florence, the lovestruck man was remote, bordering on depressed. David tried very hard to avoid Max and Thomas and hide his torment, but nothing escaped the old man's empathetic eyes. He planned to speak to his son soon if he didn't either snap out of it or go to see her in Italy.

Because none of The Songbird party had ever hunted for game before, let alone picked up a rifle, they were all clueless about the rules pertaining to the social event. As far as Max was concerned, he would have preferred to send Peter's butler to the local gun club, ask them to do the shoot and have the local butcher deliver the prepared birds to The Songbird. David had never killed anything in his life and did not feel a need to blow a bird to bits. Thomas, on the other hand, was very excited. He decided he would be satisfied just to fire a shot without killing anything, such would be the adrenaline rush of pulling the trigger for the first time.

"Roll call!" shouted Sergeant Payne.

Everyone looked at each other, wondering what to do. The novice hunters hoped the former military man was going to be in a lucid frame of mind today, rather than delusional.

"We are all here, Sarge," shouted Thomas in the hope of humouring Sid.

"Line up, men!" he ordered. "Now, who is present?"

Payne called out each man's name and insisted upon an 'aye-aye' response. Even Peter Ashwood was forced into submission.

"What the hell is going on here?" Lord Ashcroft whispered to David.

"I am not entirely sure," he replied with complete honesty.

"We have an important mission to fulfil men. Follow me and follow orders. I will keep you alive."

David took in the ridiculous situation. *How is it that four grown men were following orders from a man who had a tenuous grip on reality?*

"Attention!" shouted Sid with authority. "Forward march!"

Everybody started moving forward, guns loaded, ready to blow the first bird they saw to smithereens—game or otherwise. With military stealth, Sid lead the way turning around every so often and putting his finger to his lips, indicating for them to be silent. They would walk a little further, and then Payne would put up his hand for them to halt as he surveyed the land ahead. Peter Ashwood was becoming visibly annoyed with Sid's rigmarole. *It was my hunt. They are my guests. Yet, we have some strange fellow leading us through the woods as if we are re-enacting the Siege of Lucknow.*

It was the rustle of birds at the top of the trees that set the events in motion. The ever-vigilant Sergeant believed that he had carelessly led his men into an ambush. When he heard the wings flapping, Payne threw himself onto the ground and fired two shots at the dense evergreen rhododendrons ahead of them. Everybody watched him in confusion. He reloaded his shotgun, screaming for his men to provide cover fire, then fired another blast.

Neither Ashwood nor the others knew what to do. They crouched down, perfectly still, hoping that Payne would not fire at them with his remaining round—something they all suspected he might attempt were he to hear even the faintest snap of a twig behind him.

Eventually, tiring of the impasse, Thomas bravely began to inch forward. Sergeant Payne looked around and saw him advancing.

"Get down, soldier! Get down. That is an order," snarled Sid, jabbing his forefinger towards the frosty ground.

"Max, what the devil is this man of yours doing?" hissed Ashwood.

Max gave a shrug, then picked at a loose thread on his tweed jacket to avoid Peter's death stare. Thomas stayed on his feet, unable to face crawling along the frozen ground. Nobody said a word. They had their eyes riveted on Payne. The woods were deathly quiet. The birds had scattered at the sound of the gun. Sid was still laying on the ground on high alert.

Suddenly, a massive snow-covered branch snapped off a tree and it thundered to the ground. As loud as a gunshot, Thomas knew the sound would unsettle the sergeant. Like a scrum-half lurching for the line for the try, instantly, he dived onto the ground next to Payne, thinking he had more chance of wrestling the gun off Sid with his bare hands than dodging being shot at close range. Thomas landed heavily, winding himself.

Sid spun around and saw the young man lying motionless in the snow next to him, and he began to scream. The sound was blood-curdling and rang through the empty forest and reverberated back at them.

"No!" screamed Sergeant Payne. "No!"

He reached for Thomas and covered his body with his own. Thomas had no idea what was happening and was trying to break free of the weight on top of him. The other men looked on, not knowing what to do for the best. After quite a tussle, Sergeant Payne climbed off Thomas, studied his face and began screaming again. Sid grabbed him, pulling his head toward his chest, like a newly bereaved mother clutching a stillborn infant, crying and moaning, rocking with his eyes closed.

Max saw Sid's gun lying in the snow, and he snatched it to safety. Still distraught, Sid was holding a bewildered Thomas and tears were running down his face. It was a ludicrous, yet heart-wrenching scene. Each man had read in the papers about the heavy mental toll a life in battle can have on a soldier. At The Songbird, they had heard retired officers give vivid talks to promote their books about experiences of warfare. No one knew what to do for Sid, apart from give him time to regain his composure. They all presumed battle-fatigue and flashbacks were the cause of Sid's woes, even if they didn't quite know the precise nature of his wartime experiences and why he was suffering so badly.

Peter Ashwood was fidgeting next to David, embarrassed by what he had to witness. This was anything but the way the aristocrat had hoped the festive hunt would turn out. Slowly, Max walked over to the two men on the floor. He gently and put his hand on Payne's shoulder and spoke softly.

"Sid, it's me, Max. You're safe now. It's all over.
I have come to take you home."

Sid suddenly had a flash of reality. The soldier's face brightened, he loosened his grip on Thomas and then stood up politely. The others breathed a sigh of relief.

"Why, Max, where did you come from? I
haven't seen you for years."

His comment worried the onlookers all over again, but at least Payne was no longer armed. Max's compassionate side shone out once more.

"Let's go and have a warm cup of tea in front
of the fire, Sid. It's freezing out here. You can
tell me what you've been up to."

"Of course," answered a dazed-looking Payne,
"that would be lovely."

The Sergeant became aware of Thomas lying in the snow.

"What the hell are you doing down there, Thomas? You will freeze to death."

They were all relieved to see Sid return to the real world. Thomas had become fond of Payne, and although he did not understand what had happened in the tortured fellow's mind, he still felt deep pity for the man. The brief interval of lucidity that Sergeant Payne experienced soon evaporated when Peter shot at some pheasants. He returned to his military persona, barking orders and imagining the enemy in their midst. The whole flock flew far into the distance.

"Will Sid be alright?" Thomas asked Max.

"Yes, Thomas. If we look after him."

Peter Ashcroft, with his nerves in tatters and patience stretched paper-thin, suggested that he would ask the local gun club to help with harvesting the birds for The Songbird's Christmas menu after all.

"Great idea, old bean!" added Max with glee.

18

SID'S TORMENT

"I don't know where we'll put all this delicious food," Max said with a laugh as they sat at the table later that evening.

The planned seven-course menu was definitely a belt-buster. It was most welcome after all the exertion of trudging through the snow-covered woodland.

"We can put the leftovers in tins for the frontline soldiers," advised Sid, firmly back in his imaginary military cocoon.

Peter glared at him. *What did Max see in that crackpot?*

"Now, now, Sarge," said Thomas, "that won't be necessary, we have plenty of food at the front."

"Of course it's necessary," insisted Sid. "Here at base camp, we're well-fed, but my regiment is stuck behind enemy lines west of the Kyber Pass, and they are starving as we speak."

Ashwood watched Payne with frustration.

"Is he pulling our legs, being a bit of a wag, Max?"

"Not at all, Peter. He is earnest right now," answered Max without making any excuses. "He didn't used to be like this. He's definitely suffering more than when we first became friends. I put it down to him being fond of reminiscing, larking around a bit, but now his frontline flashbacks seem to dominate his thinking. He means no harm though, Peter, I can assure you."

Ashwood remained unconvinced. *After his antics earlier in the woods anyone can see the man's mad.*

"I will have the cooks working all night, Sarge," said Thomas gently, "but now we need to bunk down for the evening. We have a big day ahead of us tomorrow."

Before the soup for the first course was served, Thomas helped the Sid out of his seat and led him up to his bedroom. Ashwood hid a relieved smile behind his napkin, pretending to dab at his lips. David shared in Peter's thankfulness that the strange man was gone.

"Father, what were you thinking when you invited Sergeant Payne along for the weekend? I have to say his behaviour worries me."

Max noted the concern in David's voice. Ashwood took this as the cue to air his views on the matter.

"The man clearly thinks that he is still in the army. Has anyone considered putting him into an asylum? He is not in his right mind. What if he gets another gun and goes on a rampage again? The man's a menace."

Peter hoped that Jenkins had locked the gun cupboard and made a note to check himself after the meal.

"That's enough," answered Max. "If he were in his right mind, I would have left him at The Songbird, but we can all see he's not fit to be left alone for too long. Yes, he struggles at times, but he is a decorated soldier who has fought for his country. He deserves respect for that, not ridicule, Peter."

"Thomas seems to have taken a keen interest in the fellow," commented Ashwood.

"Yes, he has," Max replied. "I think at the moment, Thomas is the only person who is capable of making Sergeant Payne feel safe."

"What on earth is wrong with him? You saw him in the woods earlier, Max."

"That is how a lot of men return from war, Peter. Their minds are broken by the horrors they see."

"But not all, Max. He must have been a fragile person to begin with. Weak of mind all his life no doubt?" countered Peter.

"When he arrived at The Songbird a few days ago, he was perfectly fine. He got a bit confused when he saw the elephant at the docks, took him back to his time in India, I suppose. Then Lee Ting-Chong almost blew up the building with one of his fireworks. The shock of hearing the blast triggered a flashback. Sid thought that he was on the battlefield again and reacted in the same manner as he would leading a hundred men. He had a stand-off on the stairs with the Chinaman thinking it was another attack."

"See! The man's mad."

"Sergeant Payne led one hundred men at the Battle of Ali Masjid," defended Max.

"There were only sixteen deaths in that battle," countered Ashwood. "It was hardly a slaughter."

"You are right Peter. There were very few deaths, but unfortunately, his son was one of the sixteen. He was mortally wounded with a gunshot to the belly. The lad died in his father's arms. That's why he comforted Thomas this afternoon. It all came flooding back."

Madeleine and David watched Ashwood become remorseful, ashamed of his lack of sympathy for Sid's situation. He stared down at the table, unable to look anyone in the eye.

"It was a hellish time for him, Peter. He couldn't work as a soldier after that. Swiftly discharged, surplus to requirements. Scrapped as easily as an old tugboat. Being in the army was his lifelong ambition, and it ended horribly. He lost his mind for a while, but when he regained his sanity, he told me that he never wanted to kill another man's son ever again. He felt terrible for encouraging his lad to enter military service. His wife never forgave him, saying Sid had as good as killed their beloved boy himself."

"Max, I must apologise for my thoughtlessness."

"There is no need to apologise, only a need to understand, Peter. A little kindness in life goes a long way. He will be as right as rain in a few days, I'm sure. All he needs is a few days rest—something I thought he would have got here, but alas it seems not."

Thomas returned to the dining room.

"All's well. Sid fell asleep as soon as his head hit the pillow. Worn out with all the excitement of the shoot, poor fellow. That soup looks lovely, Mr Jenkins, I'd love a bowlful!"

As soon as the meal was finished, the young, privileged and ashamed Ashwood bade goodnight to his guests and left them sitting by the crackling fireplace in the parlour. Madeleine and Thomas turned in soon after.

David studied his father closely. It was the first time in years that they were spending time away from the business. Max was always kind and generous, but today David had seen his soul. Max had identified with Sergeant Payne's heartbreak and he wondered what his father had experienced that caused him to relate so well. Most men would have reacted like Ashwood and written Sid off as an imbecile.

"Kocham cię synu," muttered a sentimental Max in his native Polish tongue.

"I love you too, Papa."

David stood up and patted Max fondly on the shoulder then retired to his bedroom, where he would spend a sleepless night. He thought back to the love Maika had for Max and knew he felt the same way about Suzanna. *She is the one.* He was in a terrible quandary, wondering if he should go to Italy and ask Suzanna to be his wife, or let her be to follow her professional dream as they agreed. Until dawn, he tossed and turned, still unsure of the answer.

19

MONIQUE REAPPEARS

It would be Sunday morning before Monique emerged from her bedroom. Peter Ashwood was incensed by her rude behaviour, and he was decidedly cool when she appeared at the breakfast table. As usual, she looked sophisticated and beautiful. She also looked as frosty as the ground outside. To make matters worse, he had overheard a heated conversation between his fiancée and her maid. The diva reprimanded the girl for agreeing to stay in the suite and said if she was shamed by her again, she would make sure Max had her dismissed from The Songbird.

Max noticed the lover's tiff seemed to have worsened and wondered what had happened over the past couple of nights. *It seems like Ashwood might break the engagement off? Monique never would, not while she can still bask in more male attention.*

"Please meet me in my study, Monique," Peter growled.

Monique hated being summoned, and her customary feeling of defiance took hold of her. She knew her absence had offended Peter. No one believed a mere headache could incapacitate a determined woman like her for two whole days. Her mind was searching for ways to pacify the man. *Although I don't love him, being seen with an English aristocrat keeps me in the papers at least.*

"I bought this dress, especially for you," she said with a smile, twirling provocatively before him.

Peter looked at her, and he felt himself fill with disgust thinking she could win him over with such empty flattery after publicly shunning his guests since they arrived.

"Peter, mon cher! There is a problem, oui?"

She tried to run her hand down the lapel of his jacket as a sign of affection, her big blue eyes staring up at him defiantly.

"What is bothering you, mon amour?"

"You are bothering me, Monique. Your behaviour is unacceptable."

"I was so sick I could not leave my bed. You must believe me."

He could tell she was trying to manipulate him, as she was whining in the little girl voice that she used when she wanted something from him.

"Have you considered a date for our wedding yet?" asked Peter, wanting to get her on the hook and reel her in, just like he planned.

"Oh, my angel, is that what concerns you? How sweet. Unfortunately, I have not considered a date yet. As you know, I am so busy at the moment. I have no time to think. I will come back to you in the New Year. How exciting it will be to get married in the spring of a new century."

"I want to travel to France and meet your parents."

Monique stopped her coy behaviour.

"Why? What do you want with them?" she snapped.

"Out of respect, I cannot marry their daughter without their knowledge or their blessing."

Monique looked at him and pouted.

"That is impossible. Mama is ill, and Papa is abroad in Saigon."

"Are you quite sure of that?"

"Of course I am. I received a letter from my mother last week."

"We don't need to leave immediately, Monique. How about we visit France early in the new year?"

"I will be busy. You know how many bookings I have in the coming months. You have to consider my career. I have worked very hard to get to where I am in life. I can't just waltz off."

"Sit down, Monique, because what I am going to tell you may come as a shock."

For once, she obliged him without arguing.

"I wrote a letter to the De La Marre's a few weeks ago. I had it delivered directly to the chateau where your parents live."

Monique started to turn the enormous diamond engagement ring around and around on her finger.

"I received a letter back—"

He waited before he dropped the bombshell.

"—They don't know who you are. The couple has four sons and no daughters."

"That is a lie!" she protested.

"After that, I wrote a letter to every family I could find with the same surname, and none of them had heard of you except for the last woman that replied by telegram late yesterday evening."

He took a deep breath, then revealed the gist of the message.

"One of her servants had a child named 'Monique'. The woman's husband had impregnated a maid. Of course, he never admitted to it, the shame would have been too great. Much to the woman's disgust, her husband continued his affair with your mother and Madam De La Marre had to be satisfied with her husband's mistress living on the property."

"Peter you are making a grave mistake. You are accusing me of being an imposter. How dare you do that?" she screeched at him.

"The thing is, it did not matter to me, Monique."

"You would never have accepted me if you knew that first. I would not have been good enough for your family. Your parents would have chosen someone else from another blue-blooded family for you," the prima donna yelled.

"I was in love with you, your voice, your stage presence, the confident woman who appeared in public, wowing the crowd. You could have been born in Whitechapel, and I would have loved and accepted you. Look how Marie Lloyd rose from being a factory girl to the highest-paid female performer in Britain. Without a big house like this to run, she's probably wealthier than me! I promise you, your lineage would have made no difference. My family are not averse to new money."

Monique was horrified her lie had been discovered.

"I would have admired your determination and prowess, from nothing to a famous singer in the best theatre in London," he said wearily. "But that has come at a price. You have been happy to walk over everyone else to secure that position—including me."

"You cannot do this. I will ensure that the message reaches the social columns in the newspaper that I left you because you philandered."

"The men running the newspapers accept other men philandering. A quick word from me and the story will vanish without a trace. No one will care, Monique. Not in this day and age. I have witnessed your terrible behaviour towards people, Madeleine and Max in particular, and I don't want to marry you anymore. Your beauty and your voice are not enough."

"I will make you pay for this, Peter. Nobody treats me like this and gets away with it."

"I wouldn't expect anything less from you, my dear. I know that you are vicious and love to crush anyone that stands in your way."

"Our paths will cross again, and you will be sorry that you ever met me."

Monique ripped the diamond off her finger and threw it at Peter. It bounced across the floor and lay at his feet. He gave her a snide look and kicked it back towards her.

"Keep it, my dear. One day you will need the money."

Monique was proud and held her ground to start with, but her greed got the better of her once again. She sunk to her knees in front of him and picked up the ring.

"I am already sorry that I met you. All you were interested in was my family name and my fortune. You never loved me."

"Pffft! I wanted to marry well! What is wrong with that? Do you expect me to live like a peasant for the rest of my life? You do not know what it is to be poor."

"No, I don't, but I do know what it is like to be honourable."

"Do you know the phrase, Peter, that 'hell hath no fury like a woman scorned'?" spat Monique.

"Yes, I do Monique, and I also know that 'heaven has no sorrow like love turned to hate.'"

Peter had her pack immediately, then he sent her to the station to catch the afternoon train back to London. He asked Jenkins to put her in a second class compartment, taking amusement in reminding her that this time she could travel with all the common folk she despised.

20

THE RETURN TO LONDON

Later in the afternoon, Peter provided Max and his party with his best coach so they would arrive at the station in good time. Alas, when they spoke to the master, they discovered that the last train to London had been cancelled and no services would be available the following morning. Other than some sighs at the inconvenience, there were no real complaints.

The group walked to the high street and found a small hotel that could accommodate them for the night. The owner and his wife, the Maxwells, were cheerful people and happy to make them a bar snack even at that late hour. Sat in the dining room, they enjoyed a simple meal of boiled gammon, potatoes and peas, with a blob of parsley butter gently melting over it. After they had eaten, Mrs Maxwell moved them to the parlour, where they sat comfortably enjoying the peace of their surroundings.

The landlady was worried that they were still hungry. Swept up in the Christmas spirit, she supplied a plate of mince pies, gently warmed and dusted with icing sugar. Even though the dinner had been satisfying, they could not resist them. Afterwards, they drank cups of hot cocoa and stared into the firelight.

David's mind was far away. *What more did a man need?* Here they were, in a humble hotel with basic facilities, and yet they were satisfied. Life at The Songbird was stressful in comparison. He thought about Suzanna, and the simple life they could have together in Italy, living the life more of a travelling musician rather than a theatrical promoter. It did seem rather tempting. He wondered when he might broach the subject in one of the letters he promised to send her.

Sergeant Payne was back to his usual self after a relaxing walk with Max earlier in the day, and all signs of the soldier in him had disappeared. He could not remember what had happened over the last few days, just that he felt mentally and physically exhausted. From experience, Sid knew that when he entered that darkened state with no recall of events, he usually behaved strangely. He felt embarrassed and foolish in front of his new friends and his slumped position in his chair showed it.

"Stop slouching, Sid," said Max with a chuckle, "You're in good company. We care about you. That business in the wood, and the fight with Lee, it's all forgotten."

"Thank you for looking after me, Max."

"It is my pleasure. Do you remember when you saved me, all those years ago? David and I would have starved too if it wasn't for you."

In the two chairs opposite, Thomas and Madeleine had struck up a conversation and were chatting away. Max ever the romantic, took note of the budding friendship and vowed to keep an eye on the pair when they returned to the theatre.

The front doorbell tinkled, and Madeleine heard voices. She stood up and looked out of the window. The girl beckoned the others over. Mr Maxwell was offering a group of carols singers a glass of mulled wine each, the steam rising up into the night sky. They were dressed in thick dark-coloured coats accompanied by woolly scarves, shawls, hats and gloves to protect them in the freezing night. Some of the men had the lanterns hanging from long poles, with creamy-white candles glowing inside the frosted glass. Max watched as they huddled together and wrapped their hands around the cups to get some warmth into their cold fingers. Mrs Maxwell dashed out with another tray of warmed mince pies.

When they had finished their refreshments, they held their lanterns aloft and began singing again. The beautiful sound of Silent Night drifted through the crisp air. Max felt tearful. He knew the song well, having first encountered it in its native German: Stille Nacht, Heilige Nacht.

David stood next to his father and saw his eyes begin to moisten. The old man blinked hard to keep control.

"What is it, Papa?" David asked softly.

"Nothing my son. Nothing to spoil this wonderful night with."

"You are rarely melancholy especially at Christmas, Papa. Tell me what's troubling you."

"Ah, David, this joyous carol has brought back memories that I would rather forget."

By now, the music was fading and everyone in the room was listening to their conversation. They felt for Max. It was clear the song had had a marked effect upon him.

Max walked back to his seat and sat down slowly. He had a moment or two decide whether to reveal his secret. For years he kept the past from David, never wanting his son to suffer the same pain that he had. *Perhaps now is the time to tell my boy the truth.*

They all sat looking lovingly at Max. Nobody made demands upon him. There was no need to explain himself, yet the old man closed his eyes, travelling back in time to memories as vivid as if they had just happened. As he spoke, his Polish accent became a little richer.

"It was 1860, David, and I remember your mother clearly. She was the most beautiful woman that I had ever seen on the streets of 'Varshavah'—err, I mean Warsaw. It was early spring," he continued. "I cannot forget the blue dress that she was wearing. It was the colour of cornflowers, and the collar was made out of delicate white lace. I was walking behind her when she stopped to look at in a bookshop window."

Max took a deep breath. He was even further away in the past now, reliving every moment, every sensation. In his mind's eye, he watched the lovely girl stop in front of the shop. Her blond hair was pulled into a loose knot in the nape of her neck as if she didn't have enough time to style it properly. Her hat was a simple affair in contrast to some of the other's that he had seen. He watched her lean over and earnestly study one of the books at the bottom of the display. Ever the chancer, Max stopped at the window and feigned interest in the display too. She lifted her eyes from the book and smiled at the handsome young man standing beside her.

"May I ask what has caught your eye, Miss? You seem very taken by something."

"Poetry," she said with a warm smile.

"A-ha, I admire that," replied Max. "I am a terrible poet. I can't even write a letter."

"I am sure that's not true," she said before joking, "I am sure even you could manage to draw a simple 'I' or an 'O'."

Max loved the joyous playfulness in her behaviour. It made her even more attractive.

"Do you live far from here?" he enquired.

"No, Just of the market square. I live with my parents."

Max looked at his pocket watch.

"It is almost time for mid-morning tea," he announced. "Perhaps we can have some together."

"If it is at a table where everybody can see us," the girl added before rolling her eyes and sighing, "the old Warasavian women do love to gossip."

"Indeed they do. Well let's make sure we abide by their rules," Max reassured with a mischievous grin.

They chatted non-stop as they walked to a small restaurant on the street corner and took a seat outside in the warm spring sun. Excited, yet nervous, they began perusing the menu in silence before he broke the ice.

"I'm Max, Max Liebowitz."

"Maika Trzebetowsky. I'm studying at a small college for girls—much against my father's wishes."

"I work at a local theatre as a stagehand," replied Max, "—Much against my father's wishes," he chuckled. "I am sure he would have preferred that I worked down the salt mines, like a real man."

Max and Maika liked each other immediately.

"So, that is why you are roaming the streets in the mornings? You're a thespian rather than a miner. I'm glad about that, I was worried you might be one of those feckless and workshy fellows who drinks vodka all day."

Max laughed at her teasing.

"It might not sound it, but it's hard work. I begin in the afternoon and work late into the night or often the early morning. It's quite physical, moving the sets and props around between scenes."

"It sounds fascinating," enthused Maika, her eyes sparkling with interest.

"It is. One day, I am going to own a theatre, right here in Warsaw," Max said proudly. "Have you ever been to the theatre?"

"Of course I have," she laughed, "everybody goes to the theatre in Poland."

"Yes," answered Max, "I know that, but have you ever been to a real theatre?"

"A real theatre?" she asked, looking puzzled.

"It's a place where anybody can perform whatever they wish, and it does not matter where you come from, or if you are rich or poor."

Coming back to the present, Max opened his eyes and looked at his small audience in the hotel parlour.

"That is how I met Maika—your mother, David," he said.

They were all listening attentively, eager for him to continue. Settling back into his chair, Max returned to sharing his memories. *David has to know.*

"Her parents did not like me very much," he laughed. "They told her that they did not appreciate my Bohemian lifestyle. But we fell in love and over time her parents accepted me. My mother and father adored her because she brought light and joy into every situation. She was a refreshing exception to the timid and depressed creatures that roamed the streets of Warsaw—"

"—did you fall in love?" Madeleine interrupted.

"Of course, I fell in love, my dear. How could I not fall in love with such a beautiful person? She was educated, affectionate, loyal and so very full of life, always looking for the good in people and situations. Her strength of spirit was fuel for my—our—dreams. Not long after we met, we opened a café. I lived in the apartment above it. Maika stayed with her parents. At lunch, we would open our doors, and anybody was free to come in to perform and entertain. When she left college, Maika ran the café full-time. As its reputation grew, I was able to give up being a stagehand. We worked tirelessly to make the place a success. Sometimes, there were singers, other times dancers. Magicians were in abundance and acrobats—oh my, I must have seen a thousand acrobats in my lifetime. Occasionally, when we had a quiet night, Maika would get up and sing. She had an excellent voice for the eastern European styles of music, especially Slavish and Gypsy."

David shuffled forward on his seat, hanging off his father's every word.

"I would watch her and wonder what she was doing with a man like me. I asked her to marry me a year after we met, and she said yes. By then, her mother and father had realised that it was no good to try to keep us apart. They knew it was our destiny to be together. We were married in a small church in the morning, and then we went back to the café in the afternoon, where we had a party with all our wonderful friends. Our real friends, not just the people we only saw on special family occasions. We sang and danced and drank a lot of vodka—for three whole days," Max put his head back and laughed, then looked at the faces around him. "We Poles love to celebrate a wedding," he added with a twinkle in his eye.

Max seemed to retreat into his world again. He remembered their wedding night as if it was yesterday. After the party, they had gone upstairs to their apartment. They had undressed each other and laughed at their fumbling. Both inexperienced, they found themselves on a courageous journey of discovery. And what a wonderful world they discovered. If he thought that she was beautiful when she was dressed, she was breath-taking naked. She was his world, and he hers.

"Within six months, we found out that we were going to have a baby. It was going to be tough raising a child and running the café but we knew we would cope. We were lucky, since running our own business gave us a little flexibility. When you were born David, we simply carried on as usual, working day and night. We couldn't afford a nanny of course, so I build David a crib that we kept underneath the counter. No one knew our beloved son was there, although we did get some strange looks when we seemed to talk to the countertop or wave at our feet."

They all laughed. It was so typical of Max to do things differently. He grinned at them, proud of his wily and unconventional solution.

"Somehow, most nights, young David slept through all the noise without making a sound. Life was wonderful, not easy of course, but definitely rewarding."

There was a pause as the smile fell away from Max's face.

"And then our lives changed. Civil unrest threatened to overtake our homeland. The Poles, under the Russian and Prussian administrations, were to subject to ever stricter controls and increased persecution and so we sought to preserve our identity in non-violent ways. Maika and I knew things were deteriorating because there were always political discussions in the café. We drew the more revolutionary minds. Everyone knew that Poland only had a very slim chance against the opposing Russian and Prussian forces. So, Maika suggested we leave our birthplace and travel to England or America where we could begin a new life."

The sense of injustice about the way the occupation had torn through the lifestyle and business Max and Maika had worked so hard to build gnawed at David, and the others.

"At first, I didn't want to hear about the idea. I was not a coward. I didn't want to abandon my roots, nor did I want to join some sort of rebel army and get killed. I thought about it for a long time and realised that my precious little family was a tangible blessing. I loved them, and they brought me joy. I could not exchange them to fight in a war for independence which I didn't think the Polish forces could win."

All this was news to his son. Feeling betrayed, he challenged the story Max had told him in the past.

"I thought that Mama died giving birth to me," he snapped angrily. "You lied to me. What sort of father does that?"

"I had to protect you, David. I could barely live with the truth. I wanted to protect you from the pain that I felt. The answer seemed so simple and innocent at the time. I created a fantasy world for you. A place where you would be safe and happy, free from worry. The longer the lie persisted, the harder it became to tell you the truth."

David was not satisfied with the answer in the slightest, but he allowed his father to continue.

"We locked the café and left behind everything that we owned. I was told that there was a vessel sailing from the coastal city of Gdansk. We knew one of the first mates who arranged a berth for us. We were booked to sail on Christmas Eve of 1862. The three of us took a train to Gdansk and went straight to the harbour. The captain of the vessel believed that everyone would be far too busy celebrating the festive season—which meant there would be fewer soldiers patrolling the streets. I carried David and Maika walked beside me. We were going as fast as we could, without looking suspicious or so we hoped. It was freezing that night, perfectly clear, with the moonlight to guide us. With our breath formed big clouds in front of our faces, we stared at the ship thinking our new future together was about to begin. We stepped onto a pier that lead out to the moored vessels. Then a soldier stepped out of the shadows and stopped us. He blocked our way and waved a rifle muzzle in our faces."

Max took a deep breath and looked directly at David as he finally explained the secret he had kept for so long.

"Your mother knew that the foreign soldiers would either kill or torture me for information, thinking I might be part of the resistance."

"Give that woman the child," the soldier barked at me.

Your mother argued but the soldier ordered her to be quiet. She was so brave though. Before I could stop her, she tried to step between me and the rifle. She kept yelling:

"I won't let you take him! I won't!"

Max could still hear Maika screaming to this day. It was the first time that Max had ever seen her out of control. His happy, joyous soul wife was now terrified of losing her husband and was prepared to fight tooth and nail to keep him and their infant son safe.

"By now, we were surrounded by a group of soldiers. The young officer who detained us was having no success containing the situation. It was not good for his image for his subordinates to see him fail to control a mere woman. His colleagues started to smirk at him for being weak. I could see that he felt scorned."

"What happened, Papa? What happened to my mother?"

"It was a calculated decision, David. I think that they call it *malice of forethought*. The young soldier lifted the rifle and pointed it at your mother. He ensured his aim was perfect because he took his time. He was not about to be scorned by his colleagues again. Maika realised what he was going to do. I remember the shock in her face. She looked at him put up her hands. Her face was snow-white from the cold and her dry lips were pale. Her terrified eyes were the bluest that I had ever seen them."

The sense of foreboding in the story had everybody gripped with emotion. David had tears in his eyes. Max looked at his son and knew he couldn't shield him from the pain any longer.

"The soldier shot her twice in the chest at point-blank range. Because he was close to her, and the force of the bullets knocked her off the pier and she fell backwards into the icy black water. I ran to the edge and looked down. She drifted on her back for a while. Her clothes soaked in blood. Her face was now at peace, but it was a terrible sight. Slowly she drifted away. If I were not holding you, David, I would have hurled myself after her, done anything to save her—but I knew in my heart it was useless. She was gone."

Apart from the crackle of the glowing logs, the room was silent, the group hanging off Max's every word.

"I felt a pistol against my temple and they told me to run, or else they would shoot David in front of me as well. It was my turn to be terrified. I turned and ran until I got to a church where a priest preparing for the midnight mass took us in for the night."

Sid Payne shook his head sadly, remembering all too well how brutal soldiers could be.

"I had to get you out of Poland, David. The priest found a British couple who were prepared to smuggle you to England and would wait for me to fetch you. I was terrified to let you go in case I never saw you again. But what choice did I have? By now, it was January, and the Russians had overrun the country. They were hanging Polish people or deporting them to Siberia. All I could think of was that I had to reach my little boy. I dressed like a local peasant and slipped across the border into Germany. That is how I met Sergeant Payne. The British had a close relationship with the Prussians because of Victoria's marriage to Prince Albert, and some English soldiers had been stationed there. I was starving and on the verge of death. Sid overheard me asking for scraps in a bakery in Rostock, and he took pity on me."

Max looked at Sid and nodded his head in thanks.

"I told him that my tiny son was in England, and he arranged with another captain that I sail to England. I was so lucky to get his help. Lots of vessels docked at Rostock, sheltering in the deep but calm waters of the estuary before heading out to the Baltic. Sid arranged some leave to travel with me. I had nowhere to go in England, and so he made arrangements for his family to take us in for a few nights until I found work to support us properly."

Sid Payne nodded and smiled.

"I owe Sid my life," said Max.

David looked at the man whom he had enjoyed belittling in a new light. Guilty feelings now stabbed at his throat, just like they had Lord Ashwood's at dinner on Saturday.

"Please accept my thanks, too," the young Liebowitz man croaked.

"I hated Christmas after that," lamented Max. "I didn't want to see a tree or look at a church. I didn't want to hear a carol or even have a piece of Christmas cake or a humble mince pie. I raged against God wondering how he could he take my wife. I came to London and started to work at The Songbird. Every Christmas Eve, I would get so drunk that Maria, Suzanna's mother, would take David up to her quarters and look after him."

"But Max, I don't understand," wondered Thomas aloud. "These days, you love Christmas—more than all of us put together."

"I used to sit back and remember the joy that Maika had created in our in Warsaw café, and how the performances uplifted the people who visited. I started to wonder what she would want for my life. It would certainly not be drinking myself to death and neglecting our son. Eventually, I had saved enough money to buy a share in The Songbird. My elderly co-owner was childless, and I was soon blessed to discover the theatre had been bequeathed to me on his passing. He felt I would make a good job of running the place, and I worked hard to honour his memory."

Max smiled with understated pride.

"I looked for people who could benefit from my help, and that's how I ended up employing single mothers like Maria or orphans like Madeleine. Over the years, I would often go to Maria and discuss my thoughts and feelings. One day, I asked her what she thought of working at The Songbird. Well, the answer surprised me. It also turned my life around. She told me that even though we were not related, the little community of workers there were the only family that she had. I realised that the people who worked for me had nowhere else to go and that I had to give them the best experience of life that I could. That is exactly how Maika would have done it. She had the gift of creating joy for other people. So, I began to revel in the festivities at

Christmas time, to keep my Songbird family happy, and delight the audience with a magical unforgettable spectacle."

Suddenly, Max's crazy demands for the fireworks and the elephant made a lot more sense.

21

THE PROGRESS UPDATE

On Monday morning, Monique paced her dressing room restlessly. She had suffered the worst humiliation in her life with Peter Ashwood breaking off their engagement and then forcing her to return to London alone. *His audacity to investigate my past!* In her eyes, it equalled high treason. She would be delighted to put a rope around his neck and then kick the chair out from underneath his aristocratic feet.

She realised that she had underestimated Ashwood as a gormless man, and had been proved painfully wrong. *Next time, I will be more careful. A chateau in France was far too close. I will dream up something much more difficult to verify. Perhaps I shall sell myself as the daughter of a French baron living in Polynesia, wherever that is.*

*

Max left David to deal with Lee Ting-Chong and find out how the fireworks were coming along. As he wandered back to his office, he found Thomas putting up more Christmas trees with the help of the Thakur family. They were glorious specimens, filling their spaces perfectly, with their tips just an inch or two shy of the high ceilings in the theatre's corridors, dining rooms and bars. The Indian women pottered around with the decorations, 'oohing' and 'aahing' every time something bright and shiny appeared out of the box. Mr Thakur was standing precariously on the top rung of a wooden step ladder draping bunches of holly and mistletoe over every door.

The irony of the Hindu family putting up Christmas decorations did not escape Max. He was delighted they were happy and willing to help their friends. He laughed out loud and continued chuckling until he reached the Ting-Chong quarters in the attic, where relations seemed anything but warm and jovial. He gave a short rap on the door. Granny Chong opened it then looked Max up and down.

"Go! Go 'way," she scowled.

"Now, now, my dear."

Granny Chong raised her fist and lurched towards him. Max took a couple of dainty side steps to avoid her wrath and tried to peer over her shoulder to see how the work was progressing. Lee Ting-Chong came running out behind her, giving orders in Chinese. Granny Chong shook both her fists and proceeded to give him a good talking in Mandarin, then stomped off.

"Solly, Max. She velly angry lady sometime, wife's mother. You call mother-on-court, yes?"

"Mother-in-law," Max corrected him.

Lee nodded his head enthusiastically.

"Yes! Mother-in-law. I say light now," he added with a grin.

"Lee, I have come to see how the fireworks are coming along," Max said sternly.

"Ah, velly good, come," advised Lee indicating for Max to follow him. "Come look, Max. We all work hard."

Max went into the room filled with women and children sitting cross-legged on the floor. Barrels of gunpowder littered the space. In front of the workers were tiny bamboo mats that they used to roll the firecrackers. At the far side of the room, there was a gigantic pile of completed miniature explosives that were stacked up towards the roof.

"Will they work?" asked Max.

Lee nodded and grinned, very proud of himself and his team.

"We check here first. We show you now?"

"No! No!" spluttered Max, horrified by the thought.

That lot will blow this place sky high if it goes off.

"If Mr David or Mr Thomas come here, do not let them in. They will be very cross. We will keep this a secret."

"Aah," said Lee, "So, we do tiny test in theatre?"

"No, no test inside. We will use them on Christmas Day—outside!"

"Clismas too long away," argued Lee.

"You know what you are doing Lee, that is why I hired you. There is no need for a test or a demonstration. No Mr David. No Mr Thomas or they call police when they see that pile of fireworks."

The word police needed no explanation.

"No David—no Thomas—no practice—no police. I understand velly well."

"One more thing," cautioned Max.

Lee nodded, eager to please his boss.

"Granny Chong is not to smoke or cook in workroom again. Agreed?"

"Agreed, Mr Max!"

22

PRESENT SHOPPING IN THE WEST END

Max Liebowitz looked around his beloved theatre and smiled with joy. The whole building had been smothered in decorations, just as he had requested. There was nothing minimalistic in how it had been done. In fact, the base of the stage was barely visible for all the trees lining the edge of the orchestra pit. The set artists had designed nativity scenes and painted them in rich colours. The use of silver and gold leaf on the halos created a look that was more like a renaissance painting. The Songbird's owner stood speechless, taking in the beauty of it all, as his aide came to check on how the preparations were going.

"This is exactly how I imagined it, Thomas. It is perfect."

Thomas smiled at him. The compliment meant all the more after Max's revelation about Maika.

"Now, all we need is the gifts for the staff," prompted Thomas.

"Oh, my soul!" exclaimed Max. "I have forgotten about the gifts! You know how I am terrible at present shopping. How am I going to buy everything by myself?"

"I really can't help you, Max, I am, err, 'snowed under' with the final arrangements here," Thomas said wryly. "Besides, I wouldn't know what to purchase. You know the workers far better than I do."

Max knew that he was in trouble. Again. As ever, with a smile, he rose to the challenge. He paced anxiously through the kitchen, so distracted that he did not even think of greeting the staff. They watched him breeze past and wondered what their boss was up to this time. He charged down the stage doorsteps and rushed across the yard to find Sergeant Payne.

"I am in deep trouble, Sid," wailed Max. "You are the only person who can help me with this mission."

Sergeant Payne looked at Max with concern.

"Anything, my friend, anything. What is the emergency?"

"I need to go to the West End and buy gifts."

"Now wait a minute, Max," said Sid in an authoritative tone. "This is not my area of expertise. I have a contingency plan for almost any situation, but shopping is not one of them."

"Never mind that, Sid. I need help. Think on your feet, man! This is an emergency."

Max began to tot up how many presents would be required for each staff member which made him all the more apprehensive. Sergeant Payne shook his head then twirled the tips his magnificent moustache.

"I am sorry, Max, you need more specialised personnel for this task. Let me think."

Looking defeated, Max sank onto a hay bale that formed yet another nativity scene. For weeks now, he had remembered to do everything—except to buy the gifts. It was almost Christmas, and he was running out of time. He had one chance to put this right. Sergeant Payne had wandered off to what he felt was a safe distance from Max and busied himself with an in-depth discussion with Sundatara.

"Have you solved how we get that elephant onto the stage yet, Sid?" Max called out.

"Excuse me, Max! Sundatara is a lady, not 'that elephant'. You need to be more sensitive, please."

Max blinked and looked at Sid wondering if he had entered into another one of his fugue states.

"Look, Max," said Payne, "there are a few things that you need to understand about Sundatara."

Max took it as a good sign that Sid was addressing him by the correct name, rather than a military rank this time. Payne tiptoed over to Max and spoke in a whisper.

"Max, you must never use the word 'elephant' in front of Sundatara. She finds it offensive."

"She does?"

Sid glowered, annoyed his advice was being discounted.

"Oh, I wasn't aware of that," said Max looking at the beast, thinking she was very much an elephant.

The jungle beast gripped a huge tree with her strong but dextrous trunk and meticulously stripped the greenery from the branches, then delicately placed them in her mouth. Then she broke up the trunk, which Max guessed was as thick as his own leg, and chomped at the pieces until everything was gone.

"I have never seen a lady eat that much," muttered Max.

Sundatara tilted her head to one side and looked at him.

" 'Elephant' implies that she is big and fat," insisted Payne, "and it lumps her in the same category as the hordes of her unsophisticated cousins that roam Africa."

Max sighed loudly as Sid continued with his explanation.

"She is an individual. She has her personality and her problems."

The animal's big eyes stared right into Max's and she slowly fluttered her long eyelashes at him, as if she were a lady, just packaged in a different body.

"Oh, crikey, Sid! Is she batting her eyelashes at me in a seductive manner?"

Sundatara stared at Max. She extended her long trunk and pointed at his face, then sneezed violently. Max flinched in terror.

"Did you see that, Max? Do you see what happens when you annoy the lady?"

"How many more times! This is an elephant, not a debutante, Sid!" yelled Max, pressed for time and not in the mood to accommodate Payne's eccentricities.

Max wiped his face with his handkerchief, annoyed with his friend and furious with Sundatara. His mood was soon to lighten though, as Sid had a miraculous flash of inspiration.

"I know who you can accompany you on your shopping trip! The girls from Sally's! They will love to spend your money."

"Really? Do you think that they will help me? I am terrified of them. They are so—feisty!" said Max as he blushed with embarrassment.

"Of course they will help. They may be a bit rough around the edges, but their hearts are in the right place. I've known them for years. Let me have a word."

*

Max sent an already overworked Maria to see Sally's girls with an order to turn them into ladies. He thought if he could tone them down a bit, at least visually if not verbally, the shopping trip might run more smoothly. With Maria's help and a room full of costumes at her disposal, they arrived at his office looking like European royalty. Even Monique was jealous when they tottered past her dressing room.

Maria had insisted that the girls tame their hair and cover their arms. She was also adamant that they would show no cleavage, which was to be a first in many years for all of them. Maria could not afford to make one mistake in their attire or demeanour, because it would be bad enough if Max were to be seen with one 'lady of the night', let alone five. She appreciated that Max thrived on being the talk of the town, but it would be for the wrong reason if his ladies' true identities became common knowledge.

The London weather was grey and gloomy. At three o'clock the sun began to fade. The shops came alive, decorated with twinkling golden lights, and their windows filled with beautiful displays. There was a Christmas tree in each emporium, and the streets were full of merry shoppers. Max could smell chestnuts roasting, and he stopped to buy some for everyone. A bit further was a stand serving hot drinks, and Max treated his bevy of beauties to a cup of sweet warming cocoa too. He noticed when they were eating or drinking they tended to fall silent, making walking about in public less of a risk to his reputation.

Max had given up trying to remember their names, so he simply called them by the colour of their dresses: red, green, blue, yellow and pink. The women found it rather charming, having been called much worse in their chequered pasts.

"Blimey, if this is how the posh people live, I'm
never goin' back to St. Giles. Fellas seem to
have a bit more cash here," blurted out Blue.

She looked a well-dressed city gent up and down, wondering how much extra he might pay for a quick fumble in an alley.

"Cor, look at the price of that toffee there!
Three-times what I earn on me back in a
mumf," shrieked Red.

"Ooh!" cooed Green, "I'll make sweets in Sally's kitchen and flog 'em from a barra! Me finks me days of tartin' is over wif."

Max looked about, horrified, dreading their observations being overheard.

"Now, now, girls! A little less of that language or we are going home immediately," ordered Max. "This afternoon, you are ladies being escorted by a gentleman and will act accordingly. Yes?"

"Aye, Mr Liebowitz. Sorry, Mr Liebowitz," they chorused.

He heard the sound of music and steered them toward a small marching band, proudly wearing the Salvation Army uniform. Stood in a semi-circle with their instruments, they were dressed smartly against the cold in their navy and red attire. Max bent over and put money in the poor box at their feet. He nodded at the conductor in appreciation of their efforts to raise funds for the needy.

A group of children were running around a man dressed as St Nicholas beside St Martin-in-the-Field's church. It had thrown its doors open and invited the public to view an ornate nativity scene. A glittering candelabra dangled above the display, each of its arms carved into an angel, and every angel holding a candle aloft. The organ played hymns and carols in the background as the visitors took in the spectacle, discussing it in respectful whispers.

If Max were alone, he would have sat down for a while and relaxed amongst the peace of the pews. The five women stared in awe. He lit a remembrance candle for Maika and put money in the poor box once again. It filled his heart with joy to see the delight on the women's faces. He was able to give these poor ladies a day of pleasure, very much different from the pleasure to which they were accustomed.

"We ain't never going to forget this day as long as we live, Mr Liebowitz," said a grateful Yellow.

With time marching on, and very little as yet shopping accomplished, they pressed on. A determined Max marched at the front, and the ladies trailed behind like fluffy cygnets following a graceful white swan. He was on the hunt for simple but thoughtful gifts that penniless people would appreciate. The ladies were much keener to soak up the experience and dragged him into all sorts of luxury shops, none of which purveyed presents that were suitable for his budget. The freezing cold December air made sheltering inside all the more inviting. He regretted choosing the West End and wanted to move them onto another district that was a little more understated—and cheaper.

With snowflakes fluttering down from the inky black sky, Max spotted a cheery coffee shop and herded the women inside to warm up. His generosity was weakening his resolve to get the shopping done once more. He took the time to show them some whole coffee beans and explained where they came from and how they were brought to England. Instead of ordering a few biscuits, he chose petit-fours, macaroons, iced brioche buns and apricot Danish pastries. They had never experienced such delicacies or eaten in such a clean room. The ladies studied the delicate cups and saucers and giggled as they looked at their distorted reflections in the highly polished silver spoons.

The escape from the West End was going quite well until the ladies spotted a little shop in a mews, Johnson's Perfumery, they shot inside before Max could deter them. The pretty bottles stood on dark walnut shelves, French polished to shine like glass. An arrogant young man with greased back hair and small round spectacles stood behind the counter and watched the ladies with disdain. His nose was pulled up as if he had smelled something terrible.

It was Yellow who decided that she would touch one of the beautiful bottles. She lifted it off the shelf by its delicate stopper. In a flash, the fragile glass lid wobbled loose and the decorative bottle crashed to the floor, shattering on white marble tiles. Yellow stood open-mouthed, staring at the puddle of perfume on the floor. Her feet crunched on the shards of glass as she stepped back from the disaster. With difficulty, she found her tongue.

"I'm so sorry, Mister. I didn't mean to do it!"

The pretentious little fellow looked directly at Yellow with a scowl.

"That will be seven pounds," the shopkeeper sneered.

Yellow looked at the man and then turned to Max in horror.

"I ain't got that kinda money, Max," she said in a broad East End accent.

"Well then, I will have to call a constable. You cannot leave the shop without paying," warned the sales assistant, dismayed that one of the lower classes had wreaked such havoc in his luxury shop.

"Not to worry! I will settle the bill, my good man," said Max cheerfully, not batting an eyelid. "And we will buy one for you to take home, my dear. Accidents happen. No point crying over spilt milk and all that."

"You did not break the bottle, Sir. I demand payment from that—strumpet!" objected the man, jabbing his bony finger in Yellow's direction.

By his tone, it was clear to Max that the man looked down on East End women.

"Young man, it does not matter where the money comes from as long as the goods are paid for, does it not?"

"It was her carelessness that broke my precious stock. I will have her arrested, and she can battle it out in front of the magistrate."

Max could not understand what the man was trying to achieve. She had not broken it deliberately, and he had offered to pay for the damage. The salesclerk walked toward the door and Max watched him summon a bobby who was standing close by.

It was then that events took a turn for the worse.

Red, Blue, Green and Pink were infuriated by the shabby way that Yellow was treated and a small riot broke out in the shop.

"Yer a mean little sod, Mister," protested Pink.

"I know a little tight arse when I see one, yer pansy!" admonished Blue.

"You need a good fecking wallop you do," warned Red. "They would have yer guts for garters with that attitude if yer were in St. Giles."

Max froze as he watched Green ball her fist then yell:

"How about I punch yer in the gob!"

Max caught Green's hand just as she finished uttering her threat. The young constable stood in the doorway was unsure of how to get the scene back under control. Max could see that the youthful officer was inexperienced. The nervous bobby dashed outside and blew his whistle. Within seconds the shop was full of policemen.

"Look what yer done now, mate," yelled Yellow, "Yer got the bloody Peelers out didn't yer? Ye little chop!"

The police officers tried their best to calm the situation, but eventually, they were forced to arrest the five unruly women.

"Are they with you?" another constable asked Max.

"Indeed they are," he groaned.

The copper gave Max an embarrassed smile. He hadn't expected such a debonair gentleman to be associated with the East End of London. Max could hear the women yelling at the top of their voices as they were put into the police wagon. They began to beat on the side panels of the vehicle in unison and the sound thumped and echoed throughout the mews. All the pedestrians in the lane and out onto Regent Street came to a dead halt and watched the van thunder by.

"Where will you take them?" asked Max.

"To Westminster police station, Sir."

"Are the courts still open to hear cases of affray today?"

"Yes, Sir."

Max looked thoughtful. *Perhaps the bailiff can arrange a session immediately?* He sent a young lad with instructions to go to The Songbird, ask for David, and give him a note which read:

'Meet me at Westminster Magistrate's Court. ASAP. PS Bring lots of money, I may have need of it for a bribe.'

David read the note and left immediately, bringing Thomas along for moral support. He had a horrible feeling his father had got himself into hot water again.

The magistrate was in a hurry to get to his club and have a drink. He had been an alcoholic for years and struggled to make it past three o'clock without some of Scotland's finest. To expedite proceedings, he swore the five women in at the same time. After everybody said their 'I swears' and 'I dos', the sorry lot of them each gave their versions of the story, each one a little more far-fetched than the previous tale. None of the bobbies could help, having not seen the bottle break or the initial events that lead to the escalation of the dispute. The magistrate wondered if he would ever get to the truth of the matter. Eventually, he called Max to the stand.

"Mr Liebowitz, I am struggling to make head or tail of this affair. Will you please tell me what happened? You seem to be the sanest person in my courtroom."

"It is simple, your Honour. Yellow over there broke a glass bottle of perfume by accident. The shopkeeper got rather hot under the collar when he heard that she was from the East End. I offered to pay for the damage, but he refused payment. That was when Green, Blue, Pink and Red became involved. They wanted to defend their friend, thinking the matter was easily resolvable and the man was being petty and vindictive."

"It makes sense you offered to make good for the breakage," the magistrate agreed as he wondered why this rabble was even in front of him.

"The shop keeper took an inexplicable dislike to Yellow from the minute she tried to apologise. They felt it was absurd that I couldn't pay on her behalf."

"I see. So, Mr Johnson, to resolve this matter swiftly, you will accept payment from Mr Liebowitz. Is that understood?"

"Yes, your Honour," agreed the perfumier begrudgingly.

"Yellow, you are innocent. You did not deliberately break the bottle."

"Yes, your majesty. I mean your Honour—
Lord—Sir," whimpered the relieved woman.

The judge stared at Green for a while.

"Green, I recognise you from somewhere," he
said. "Have you been in this courtroom
before?"

"No, your Honour," she replied knowing that
he probably remembered her from his
numerous visits to Sally's to partake in some
rather racy services.

"Good, Green. We do not need repeat
offenders."

"Ladies, your raucous behaviour in a luxury
store this afternoon was appalling and must
have cost Mr Johnson considerable business at
this time of year. However, I can empathise
with your frustration about the harsh
treatment of Yellow. You get away with a
warning. I don't want to see you in this
courtroom again. Do I make myself clear?"

"Yes, Sir. Thank you—and Merry Christmas!"
they cheered.

"Get out of here, Mr Johnson. You have wasted
the court's time and mine. In future, if a
customer offers to pay for their breakages, I
suggest you accept that offer with good
grace."

Max gave a sigh of relief while David and Thomas stood at the back of the courtroom, amazed by what they had just witnessed. The bailiff herded them out of the courtroom and close the door behind them.

"Your Honour, do you wish me to document your judgement?"

"Don't be stupid, Mr Barclay, go home. I need to be at my club in ten minutes, or I may have a breakdown."

23

FLORENCE

Suzanna sat alone in her room. She had imagined Italy to be bright, sunny and warm. Instead, it was dark and wintery. That afternoon, Florence was as gloomy as London. The Italians were caught up in the yuletide festivities, leaving Suzanna to fend for herself. She had little idea about the continental customs of the season, which made her feel incredibly homesick and craving a small slice of familiarity.

The room was chilly and bare because the Italians had the attitude that the view over the city should be sufficient to impress any visitor, and comfort was a distinctly secondary consideration.

The villa was empty, save for a few lost souls like Suzanna who had nowhere to go for Christmas. The audition process was a lot slower and more arduous than she anticipated. The two French sopranos that were in permanent residence were as arrogant as Monique. Suzanna began to understand that rudeness was not exclusive to the Songbird's Gallic diva. *I have no doubt it is a French custom.*

Since she arrived, Suzanna's passion for her opportunity had waned. She began to question if she had entered the competition because she desired to be a famous soprano—or because she wanted to beat her nemesis, Monique. She was embarrassed to admit that winning had given her far more satisfaction than singing scales over and over again, or struggling to overcome the language barrier.

Time alone in Italy had matured Suzanna. A date was still to be set for her audition, and the likelihood of even a bit part in the première of Tosca in the new year was fading fast. All her life she had dreamed of an opportunity to perform. Now it was within her reach, it didn't feel as good as she hoped. Melancholic, listless, and alone, she wanted to return to the safe and happy haven where she was raised and be her loving mother and surrogate Songbird family once more.

Suzanna stared out of the window, taking in the view of one of the most beautiful cities in the world. A tear of self-pity ran down her face. Lost about what to do next, she climbed into bed and pulled the blankets over her head, doing her best to shut her surroundings out. All that did was remind her how unhappy and alone she was. She had still not received a telegram from David as promised. Her work schedule was so punishing she didn't have time to find out how and where to send one to him. *Why has everything gone so wrong?*

Monique had not accepted being judged second best at the competition and never would. The diva's initial wrath had become a fully-fledged vendetta against Suzanna. It was time to use the only tool that Monique had left to ruin her foe's singing career. If Monique had been closer to the judges on the night of the contest, she would have used her body. Now, she had to use her wits. The chanteuse decided to see David, hoping she could persuade him to help her with the plan to bring Suzanna's future crashing down.

David sat at his desk and stared at Monique. She was the last person that he expected to see. He gauged from her expression that it was not a friendly visit. Mentally, he prepared himself for yet another confrontation. *What the hell does the woman want now?*

"May I sit down?" asked Monique.

"Is it urgent?" asked David, trying to find a reason to dismiss her.

"Oui," she confirmed as she settled into the chair before his invite to take a seat. "As you know, Suzanna stole my opportunity to go to Florence."

Just the word Suzanna cut through his heart. As the Christmas show loomed, David did not have time for Monique's endless selfish whining. Tired, overworked and miserable, it was the last thing he wanted to hear.

"I have a little surprise for you, David," said the starlet in her husky French accent. "Some information that I will use if you do not bring Suzanna home immediately."

Now she had David's full attention.

"I know Suzanna's secret and I will use it against her."

"Please, Monique, get to the point. I have no time for your cloak and dagger antics today."

"Suzanna's father is a Gypsy, a dirty traveller. That is why she has dark skin. Her mother was a tramp and went with him like it was nothing. She was with child when she arrived here—unmarried."

Motionless, David started at the woman in front of him. She was the ugliest person that he had ever met—inside and out. Monique was surprised that he was not reacting to the news. Frustrated by the lack of response, she became more venomous.

"Max knows about her sordid past but he covered it up with Maria to deceive you. They were in it together for over twenty years. Everyone knows the Romanies are bad people and not to be trusted. This news will ruin your business. The English rose everyone took to their hearts is really a vile foreign Gypsy. It will shut your doors," she threatened David.

David stared at her, disgusted.

> "This is no surprise to me, Monique. I know everything about Suzanna since childhood. We grew up together and have no secrets."

It was not the response that the diva was expecting. She changed tack with a spiteful attack.

> "I saw you take her to your apartment the night of the firework explosion," she yelled. "I stayed awake, and I waited to see when she would return. I had to wait all night, but it was worth it to know you bedded her."

Thomas and Max heard Monique shouting and hurried to David's office, listening to every word of the shrew's accusations wafting through the door.

> "It proved to me Suzanna Stratton is a Roma tart just like her sinful mother, Maria," screeched Monique.

The two men stared at each other wondering whether to interrupt. David could not control himself any longer. He sprang from his chair like an enraged lion and grabbed her by the throat. He was so powerful she was swiftly dragged out of her seat. His hands clamped around her throat and mouth. Crying for help was not an option.

"How will it feel when you can never sing again?" David threatened as he began to crush her windpipe.

The door swung open and Thomas saw Monique's arms flailing as she fought to breathe.

"Stop it, David! Stop! You'll kill her!" Thomas roared as he tried to pull David away.

Finally coming to his senses, David released Monique, and she slid down to the floor gasping for air. Max was in no mood to show the harpy any compassion.

"Get up, Monique. I want you to leave immediately."

"You can't do this to me. I have been loyal to you and filled this place night after night. Your son just assaulted me and I will be going to the police," she rasped.

"Do as you see fit, Monique, but I never want you near this theatre again," Max told her coldly.

"This place is finished. I will see to it."

"There are many women as talented as you are. Suzanna has shown us that."

At the mention of Suzanna, Monique went wild again.

"I am trying to protect David from her!"

David lurched forward and Thomas had to intervene once more to stop him throttling her.

"Get out!" shouted Max. "We never want to see you again."

Thomas took Monique by the arm and marched her to the door and shoved her through it. Nobody backstage said goodbye to Monique. She had to find help off the street to carry her trunks. After her departure, The Songbird was deathly quiet. The staff had never witnessed such wrath from their normally charitable employer.

*

Monique booked into the cheapest dreariest hotel she could find in the West End. After trying to rally support from her wealthy friends, she found none of them could accommodate her. They were either off to their country houses or entertaining house guests in the city over the festive season. Nobody wanted to take responsibility for a social leech.

For the crestfallen star, there was only one option left. In her heart, she knew that it would not make a difference to her predicament, but she decided to do it out of spite. At the grubby hotel desk, she began to write a barbed letter to the Ambassador Francesco de Renzis and marked the envelope with the word 'Urgent'.

When the letter arrived on the ambassador's desk, he noted on the back it was from Mademoiselle De La Marre. He ran his nose along the edge of the correspondence and closed his eyes as he smelled the expensive French fragrance. The ambassador was delighted. The singer looked stunning and he was eager to meet her. Bored by his wife for years, the blonde beauty would provide the perfect distraction he needed to survive dull London.

The information that Monique had forward to him was alarming. Having served in the diplomatic corps for many years, and he knew that there was some substance to the Romany threat. Best of all for him, he knew if he ruined Suzanna's future, a grateful Monique would be his enthusiastic lover for as long as he was posted in the English capital.

24

LASTMINUTE PREPARATIONS

"I refuse to sew Sundatara a tutu," grizzled Maria. "I have too much work to do as it is. Besides, where am I going to find the material to do it. She is huge! Do you want me to cut up the stage curtains?"

Max looked at Maria, knowing that she would not budge. He gazed around the workroom to see who was idle.

"And none of my girls are free to do it either," she told Max fiercely.

"I agree with Maria," said Sid. "Why do you want to cover the beautiful Sundatara?"

"She will be a glorious novelty in a skirt," countered Max, his face lighting up as he imagined the scene.

"Don't let her hear you. She will take offence. Sundatara doesn't need any enhancements to draw a crowd. She is perfect as she is."

Max sighed. He was outvoted, two to one. He had great respect for Sid's advice when it came to the beast mainly because he did not want Sundatara sneezing on him again.

"Thomas, do you know how are we going to get Sundatara onto the stage?" asked Max. "Do we have a solution yet? We don't have long and we seem to be going round in circles."

The young aide shook his head.

"The chippies have said the stage will never hold Sundatara. She is too heavy—."

"—well built," Sergeant Payne corrected him.

"—too heavy for the joists," Thomas insisted. "And in terms of access to the stage—"

"That is not acceptable. You must come up with an idea!"

"I have. I need to break a hole in the sidewall, build a ramp and reinforce the stage," he snapped.

"Must it be so complicated?" asked Max, who had no practical knowledge of woodworking or building works.

"Unfortunately, yes Max."

"Why do I feel like everyone and everything is against me?" wailed Max. "This is the greatest show of my career, my swansong, and every time I request something, the answer is 'no!' Is this a conspiracy?"

"I thought you said last year's show was the greatest," disagreed David.

Max gave David a foul look. As much as he loved his son for his financial acumen, he still had no idea how to put on a true spectacle. *He knew business—but not show business.*

"What are our alternatives?" demanded Max.

"We can parade her in front of the theatre," suggested Sid.

"By Jove, no!" exclaimed David. "That big lump will trample someone to death."

"Stop that immediately, Max. I won't have you insulting Sundatara. We have become very close."

David could not believe what he was hearing. Everyone around him was mad. Secretly running off to some remote country hotel over Christmas was becoming an ever attractive option.

"Well then, you think of something, Sid," replied David in defeat.

"Why not parade her down the auditorium's main aisle? That's nice and wide," proposed Max.

"But what about the mess? Who will clean it up? Not to mention the smell," David said with a grimace.

"Sundatara does not smell," snapped Payne. "Mr Thakur washes every day and she smells like patchouli."

"Never mind that," David reprimanded. "Are you going to walk behind her and collect her droppings?"

"Golly, no!" said the soldier. "I thought that Thomas could do that."

Thomas looked stunned.

"And what do we do with the droppings when Thomas has collected all of them?"

"I pondered that very seriously. I have an answer," announced Payne confidently.

David raised his eyebrows and braced himself for Sid's next big wheeze.

"We can sell it a fertilizer. Fertilizer is big business. We'll make a fortune."

"That settles it," said Max excitedly. "Well done, Sid. What an excellent idea."

"Over my dead body," warned David. "I can't believe you would consider such a ridiculous plan. The theatre will be wrecked for a few shillings in return."

Once more, it was Thomas who provided the solution that satisfied all the rival demands.

"Sarge, Max, I have the perfect answer," he said with a cheeky grin. "We know that Sundatara is a very proud woman, and her image means everything to her. I suggest that we decorate the courtyard with pretty Christmas lights and trees. Let's allow people into her enclosure to feed her clementines. I am sure that she will be delighted with extra rations, and they will be in awe of being so close to such a magnificent animal. The children will remember it forever."

The men looked at each other and began to nod their heads. It was the best plan so far, and David was relieved when Max agreed to it.

*

"Max, while I have you with me, Lee Ting-Chong is asking for more heat in his rooms, he says that the children are cold," counselled Thomas.

Max didn't say a word.

"Lee says Granny Chong does not have enough coal for her stove up there."

"She can cook in Mrs Bowles kitchen," answered Max, unable to look Thomas in the eye.

"And Lee says that the children are hungry."

Usually, anything pertaining to the welfare of children got Max's attention, but he just stared into the distance pretending that he had not heard Thomas. Max was terrified. He had seen the fireworks piled up to the ceiling, and he knew that Granny Chong had almost blown the attic to bits. *That woman cannot be trusted.*

"What are you hiding from us?" asked David.

Max looked sheepish.

"Oh no, Max, this has something to do with the fireworks, doesn't it?" asked Thomas.

"They are piled to the ceiling Thomas, and if Granny Chong persists with cooking next to them, she will blow up this building."

"And ruin Sundatara's introduction to show business."

"To hell with that blasted elephant!"

Sid was about to come to Sundatara's defence, but Thomas would not hear of it.

"I don't want a word from you, Sarge. You are the only man here familiar with explosives. Get up to the attic and find a safe place to store those bloomin' fireworks. I want it done immediately."

David began to laugh. He had never believed that mild-mannered Thomas had it in him to take control of a situation, but he was wrong. It seemed Thomas was more than able to run The Songbird. *Perhaps I should go to be with Suzanna after all, if I am not needed here?*

Over in Grosvenor Square, Francesco de Renzis sent a telegram to the musical director in Florence giving the details of Monique's complaint and advised that Suzanna should return to London immediately to preserve the good standing of the opera.

25

THE AUDITION

The opera's director of music summoned Suzanna to his office. A small grey-haired man, full of self-importance, he had been raised by a demanding father who had no time for women. The director's view of them worsened when he became stuck in a loveless marriage. His only meaningful interaction with females was when he needed the services of a brothel. For the best part of a year now he had been so busy planning the production of Tosca, which meant the opportunities for his flesh to be satisfied had been few and far between.

"Sit down," he ordered Suzanna.

She complied, terrified, having heard several rumours about how awful the director was if he were angered.

"You have been dishonest with us," he continued.

Suzanna was taken aback by the accusation.

"How so?"

"I have received a telegraph from London. Read it," he told her as he threw the note across his desk. "Is this true?"

"Yes, it is," was the meek reply.

"Why did you not inform us about this?" demanded the director.

"I didn't think it was applicable. I thought that people are chosen for their talent, not their parentage," answered Suzanna.

"We cannot have a Roma amongst our students. They will never tolerate it," he said abruptly.

Suzanna stared at him in disbelief. For the first time in her life, Suzanna experienced anger as she never had before. How dare this oily little man sit in front of her and critique her life. She was proud of who she was, and she did not have to excuse herself.

"I participated in the competition. Your judges chose me. I am not to blame for this," she argued courageously.

The director studied Suzanna's determined face. He had heard her singing, and there was no doubt that she was very talented and an asset to the Italian opera school.

Italian men did not fall far from the hedonistic Roman tree. He weighed up the pros and cons of keeping

Suzanna in Florence. His conclusion was the same as the ambassador's about Monique. *If I ensure the girl stays at the school, she will have to show me her appreciation.* He stood directly in front of Suzanna leaning against his desk. He felt a stirring for the first time in months. If this was his reaction just looking, he wondered how aroused he would he feel in bed with her.

"Are you lonely in Italy?" he said, trying to
sound gentle, but it came across sinister.

Suzanna did not answer him, feeling uncomfortable with him so close to her. It was thoroughly inappropriate. He bent forward and stroked her cheek gently, his head mere inches away from hers.

"I can help you stay here and become our
most famous soprano. I will keep your secret
safe," he whispered.

Suzanna's eyes narrowed, knowing that he was going to stipulate his conditions.

"You will have to look after me, of course,
Suzanna. I am all alone in the world, just like
you. If you want to sing for the opera, the
answer is very simple. We don't need to
bother with a formal audition. This will do—"

He reached towards her bosom, groaning with pleasure as he approached. Suzanna jumped to her feet then slapped him so hard across his face his ears rang.

"What do you think you are doing, you stupid woman?"

"I have a home, and I have a family—and I have a man who loves me."

In a furious temper, Suzanna packed her necessities into a carpet bag and marched to the station. She had never felt more confident in her life. She was in love with David and regretted that she had chosen Italy over him. Nothing was worth it if she did not have him in her life. She did not know how long it would take to reach London, but she was not afraid to find her way home, back to the man that she loved.

26

NARENDRA

"Mr Thomas! Mr Thomas! We have a terrible problem," Mr Thakur shouted as he ran across the courtyard.

"Narendra Thakur has disappeared," he yelled.

"You've lost one of your children?" asked Thomas, readying himself to jump into action.

"No, Mr Thomas. Narendra is the snake."

"What snake?"

"The snake for the show, Mr Thomas. My brother in law is a snake charmer and he says Narendra has disappeared."

"Is it dangerous?" asked Thomas.

"Yes! Narendra is a cobra. "

Thomas closed his eyes in horror. Even the English knew that a cobra bite was deadly. The kerfuffle attracted Max's attention.

"What's all this racket? What's happening now?"

"Narendra is missing, Mr Max."

"Oh my goodness, Thomas," said Max, "Panic stations. Call Sergeant Payne, he will know what to do."

Payne divided all the men into small groups and told them where to search, suggesting they each went off armed with a club or a spade.

"Capture Narendra alive," ordered Sergeant Payne. "We cannot afford any fatalities."

A man wearing a top hat crossed the courtyard and approached Thomas purposefully. It was the magician, The Great Maurice, who still resembled an undertaker.

"Mr Thomas," he warned, "I will hold you personally responsible if that snake kills Judas."

"Who's Judas?" asked Thomas.

"One of my disciples."

Thomas looked utterly confused and gave Maurice a look that suggested now was not the time to be obtuse.

"He's my white rabbit—and the cornerstone of my act," hissed the magician. "Frankly, I do not know where he is—and woe betide you if he is inside a snake's belly!"

"Is there no way you do can your show without Judas?"

"Perhaps you'll have me magic up the elephant from my top hat. That will be a crowd-pleaser for Max," Maurice said sarcastically. "Judas has been by my side for years. He loves to wander off and explore backstage but always returns before the show. It's not been a worry in the past, but knowing that blasted snake may prey on him—I am terrified."

David arrived in the courtyard, also eager to see what all the fuss was about.

"We need to be sensitive," said Max, panicking, "these creatures are precious to their owners."

"I saw a white bunny outside Lee Ting-Chong's door," said David. "Perhaps you should look there first?"

Max stood to attention.

"Leave it to me, Maurice. Please stay here. Can't be too careful with this cobra on the prowl. Rest assured, Sergeant Payne and I will find Judas for you."

Sid and Max bounded upstairs. Curiosity compelled Thomas, David and Mr Thakur to follow. Fretting about his beloved Judas, Maurice ignored Max's instruction and tagged along at the rear calling out the rabbit's name. Judas, however, was nowhere to be seen. The magician went to check on the remainder of his livestock housed in one of the attic's many cubby holes close to Lee's lodgings.

Payne knocked loudly on the Chinese workers' door. Lee opened up and peered through the gap. Beads of sweat began to form on Max's brow, and not just because of the exertion of climbing several flights of stairs in one go.

"What wong, Mr Max?" asked Lee.

"We are searching for a white rabbit," Max probed. "Have you seen him?"

"I see labbits often. They hop hop hop on steps."

Maurice returned looking a little more at ease.

"Simon, Peter and Andrew and the others are safe in their straw beds," the magician announced, relieved. "Alas, Judas is still at large."

"How many rabbits do you keep up there?" asked David.

"Twelve!" Maurice tutted. "They are disciples, man! Have you been listening to me at all? They follow me religiously. That's why my wife suggested apostles, but I preferred disciples."

That comment alone confirmed to David they were dealing with another mad man. Granny Chong appeared behind Lee, brandishing a bloodied meat cleaver, looking more cheerful than usual.

"Granny Chong make special dinner tonight," said Lee proudly.

The blood drained from Maurice's face.

"Oh, how lovely," said Max cheerfully, forgetting Granny Chong's propensity to light the fireworks with a stray spark from her stove. "Sharing a hearty meal is a special time for families," he gushed.

"What will she be cooking?"

Lee looked at Granny Chong and spoke to her in Mandarin. The old woman beamed in delight, then jabbered a swift response before disappearing back inside.

"She bling meal to show you, Max. She good cook."

Moments later, Granny Chong returned, smiling from ear to ear. In one hand, she carried Judas by his ears furiously wriggling as if his life depended on it, and in the other one, she had an angry and muscular Narendra firmly by the neck, his tail whipping around furiously with contempt.

Maurice and Mr Thakur ran forward at the same time. The old woman could not work out what all the fuss was about. She stepped behind Lee and shouted at them, refusing to hand over their precious pets. Maurice manhandled Lee out of the way, reached for Judas and started to pull at his legs, desperate to free the animal. Mr Thakur clutched at Narendra's long body. A frenzied tug of war ensued. Feeling she was being attacked, Granny Chong shrieked in terror and tightened her grasp.

Sergeant Payne could predict what would happen. Granny Chong would be left with Judas' ears, and Mr Thakur would be left with a headless snake stretched to twice its length. It was time for the military man to regain control of the troops.

Sid reached into his top pocket and pulled out a whistle. The shrill sound was so piercing everybody covered their ears with their hands. The two creatures fell out of Granny Chong's hands, with their owners diving forwards, desperate to halt their fall. Her gnarled hands grasped like the talons of a bird of prey, angry her quarry had been stolen and her meal plans ruined. Lee had to give her a bear hug to restrain her as they made their escape.

Downstairs, Max was the first to speak, acting as if the chaos was perfectly normal.

"Right then. That's all sorted. Good-o. Shall we get back to working on the Christmas show fellas?"

27

THE CHRISTMAS EVE SPECTACLE

David sat in his apartment and looked across the street to The Songbird. The last few days had been the worst in his life. Aside from the continual demands of the business, his life was empty. He missed Suzanna far more than he thought he would. Their romance had been brief and fleeting and he expected to move on quickly. What he hadn't anticipated was the intensity of it. *She's the one. I know she is. And now she's gone.*

The Christmas chaos at the theatre seemed to spiral more and more out of control each year. He was exhausted with it all. Although his father had said he would step away when he retired, David couldn't quite see Max abandoning his crazy showbiz schemes— especially now he knew how much it mattered to Maika.

After many a sleepless night, David made a decision. *I will continue to be an accountant, but for a business with a more stable and measured owner—someone who values budgetary restraint, cash reserves and respects my financial projections.* He would find a small house somewhere in the countryside, a short train ride from a town or city. He would fall in love and finally give Max his darling grandchildren. Alas, despite being certain on his professional future, he was not yet ready to abandon his dreams for a life with Suzanna, although he knew at some point he would have to. There had still been no word from her since she left.

David was annoyed that he did not tell her his feelings sooner, that he wanted her to be part of his future more than anything else. His heart had broken when he said goodbye to her. The night she departed, he had gone to his apartment and got roaring drunk. He threw the empty whiskey bottle into the fireplace. Halfway through the second bottle of single malt, he collapsed onto his bed.

The temptation to go to Florence and find her was strong, but he preferred that she contact him first. If she had fallen in love with her new singing career, he knew his attempts to woo her would be doomed. He toyed with the idea of sending a telegram to at least wish her well in her forthcoming debut but had struggled to find the time.

The joy of Christmas escaped him most years, and this year he positively hated it. *I have no interest in these blasted festive shows. This year has been a farce from the outset. If I had my way, I would sleep through all of December and wait for the dreadful thing to pass.*

With the disgraced Monique now dismissed, Max had to source a new singer in a hurry. He put a bold quarter page advert in The Times advertising the vacancy. He was inundated with applicants. Fortune smiled upon him and the audition brought forth another beautiful woman with a powerful voice. The moment that Max heard her, he knew she would succeed. The songstress jumped at the chance to fill Monique's shoes and began rehearsing in her lodgings the day she heard she was successful.

David heard a knock on at his door. Thomas had come to check up on his missing colleague.

"Why aren't you dressed? We only have an hour to go to tonight's show!"

"I am not going," muttered David, looking a little tipsy.

"You must go. It's Christmas Eve. Tonight is one of the biggest nights."

"No, Thomas. Tomorrow is the big charity day. I will go tomorrow instead."

"You know how significant tonight's show is to your father."

"It has no meaning for me. I am tired of Christmas. I am tired of The Songbird. And even though the theatre is heaving with people—I am lonely."

"Well, you won't be lonely if you're with us
over the road. Come on, now."

Thomas was in no mood for any more Leibowitz
shenanigans. In silence, he selected an outfit and lay on
the bed ready for David to put on, but he didn't take the
hint. Thomas began to dress him like a girl would dress
a dolly, trying to pull his limbs about and force them into
his evening suit. It was no use. He let David flop back
onto his bed. The mournful man sat with his head in his
hands as if he were hiding from the world. Thomas
waited a few minutes before he spoke.

"This morose attitude of yours of late, it's
because of Suzanna, isn't it?"

David nodded.

"Yes, it is all because of her. She has been the
greatest joy in my life, Thomas. I have known
her for so long, and I don't know how I will
live without her."

"I guessed you were keen on her. It seems my
hunch was right."

"Papa had an inkling too, but it was Monique
who was certain of my feelings to Suzanna."

"Is that why you attacked her? Because of her
diatribe about Suzanna's father?"

David nodded.

"Before the competition, I decided I was going to ask Suzanna to marry me. I even bought a ring. I think we both secretly thought Monique would win."

David dragged open one of his desk drawers and pulled out a small velvet jewellery box. He tossed the case over as if it were nothing. Thomas opened it. Inside, a stunning diamond solitaire glistened.

Not knowing what to say, he clicked the box shut and respectfully returned it to David, who slid the small box back in his inside pocket.

"Come on, old chap. You don't have to make a big show of it tonight. Just let Max know that you are there and give him some peace of mind. He'll worry if you're absent."

"No, Thomas. Not tonight. I want to be alone with my thoughts. I will force myself to attend tomorrow."

Thomas poured the two of them a glass of whiskey, sensing that David needed some moral support. He was sure he could salvage the situation, even though the atmosphere was tense. Silence reigned. David sank into his loneliness once more. It absorbed him like quicksand. Thomas couldn't see a way to change his mind and gave up, vowing to try harder tomorrow.

"Look, we have a busy night ahead. I need to get going. I'll tell Max you are feeling unwell but I am sure he'll know that's a lie. I'll check up on you later.

From his apartment window, David watched the sophisticated crowds arrive in their fancy carriages and glittering gowns, but it made no impression. There was nothing that represented Christmas cheer in his apartment. It was bare, cold, joyless and loveless.

The lovestruck man poured himself another drink and sat next to the fire. He fell asleep on his chair, only to be awoken by the sound of fireworks at midnight as the audience left. He did not even bother to look out of the window and admire them. He got into his bed fully clothed, pulled his covers over his head and tried to sleep.

28

THE BIG DAY ARRIVES

Max delivered a three-line whip to Thomas to act as his henchman. *David will be forced to attend our show on Christmas Day and that is the end of the matter.* For Max, it was his swan song party, and there was no way he would tolerate his son's absence. Even though the Christmas Eve show had been chaotic behind the scenes, David's failure to appear had not gone unnoticed by his father.

It was almost three o'clock in the afternoon, and Thomas advised David he had to hurry to be on time, else there would be no limit to his father's wrath. David washed and dressed as fast as he could, giving himself a pep talk as he stared in the mirror. *Come on, you can do this, David. One last time—then you can tell him you're leaving. The Songbird will be safe in Thomas' hands.*

For someone who was in such a hurry, David arrived at The Songbird looking exceptionally well turned out. The air was crisp, and the dark clouds hung low. There was a good chance of snow.

He pushed his way through the unruly crowd of working-class locals, to whom the day was dedicated. As he arrived at the front entrance lots of girls nudged each other and pointed at the tall and handsome blond man passing by. David pushed his way into the crowded foyer then through to the theatre looking for Max. He found him and Thomas stood in the main aisle watching everyone find their seats, greeting each person with beaming smiles.

"Ah, Thomas, my man! Look at that! Have you ever seen so many happy faces? Oh, how I wish Maika could see this. She would have been overcome with pride."

The theatre was a brilliant display of twinkling yellowy lights, contrasting wonderfully with the red velvet seats. What was left of the Christmas trees decorated the auditorium wonderfully.

David joined the two of them. Max put his arm around his son's shoulders and hugged him.

"Come with me, I have something special to show you," he said, before proudly escorting his son towards the stage door. "Your mother would have loved what I have done."

This something special—can it be Suzanna? Maybe that's why I didn't hear from her? She's been travelling back?

In the courtyard, Thomas had created a miracle. It looked like a winter wonderland, and the underprivileged locals moved through it in wonder. Stands were supplying roasted chestnuts, piping hot mince pies and steaming cups of cocoa. The atmosphere was one of joy and excitement. Thomas had set a large Christmas tree in each corner and strung lanterns between them, creating a carnival-like atmosphere. David looked furious.

My father means that damned elephant!

David watched Sundatara standing in the middle of the adoring crowd, sensuously blinking her long eyelashes and accepting all the delicacies that Sergeant Payne handed out for them offer.

> "She has the same vanity as Monique, but she
> is far more pleasant to deal with," joked Max.

Max and David went to stroke the trunk of the beast. She was a huge draw for the event had certainly earned her keep. Sundatara's inquisitive trunk patted at David's suit, thinking the lump in the inside pocket might be a clementine. David pushed her away worrying she might sneeze all over him. The father and son watched the delight of the crowd who had never experienced a spectacle like it.

> "This is why I love Christmas," said Max,
> surveying the people. "It is an opportunity to
> make dreams come true, Son."

My dream won't though. David felt ashamed of his sudden selfishness. The ragged people around him had nothing but they were still filled with joy. *I have so much to be grateful for. I shouldn't feel maudlin.* As more snowflakes began to fall, the awestruck children looked skyward, mouths wide open, trying to catch one on their tongue. It was such a simple pleasure, but they giggled with delight as they felt a tiny spec of cold land and then melt away. Each tiny face looked at their parents, who grinned down at their child with pride.

Inside, some brass bells rang out.

> "The show is going to start, David! Let's go in. This is going to be a night to remember for us, just as much as them. Thank you for your tireless support. I know I can be difficult to work with, but I do value your loyalty. And just look at what we can achieve when we set our hearts on it!"

Thinking back to his musing about the plan to leave The Songbird behind, guilt pricked at David's conscience.

Sally's girls opened the show, dressed as burlesque dancers. Lacking inhibition, they were comfortable bending down and displaying their knickers or kicking the legs in the air. The display was rather risqué for a family audience, but no-one seemed to mind. The lyrics to their songs had the crowd in stitches. Even curmudgeonly David had to smile. He was surprised at how well they could sing and dance in such a short time. He had a sneaking suspicion that Max would retain their services in the long term. He turned to look at his father who was clapping along to their songs enthusiastically, looking more like a young apprentice than a grizzled retiree. *I am sure he will never leave this place! He's part of the fixtures and fittings.*

His amazement continued as he watched the little Ting-Chong children demonstrating their considerable acrobatic skills. It was no wonder that they could jump over the balconies and hang from ropes without killing themselves. They flipped each other into the air to form a human pyramid five levels high. From a standing start, they could somersault on to wooden boxes twice their height, then do a double somersault on the way back down. The crowd whooped with delight as each boy leapt up.

At the end of their act, David watched Granny Chong escorting the acrobats off the stage, waving her matronly fist in the air, else the little bundles of Chinese energy would have never stopped. Once the curtain closed, they ignored her and scattered in every direction, determined to enjoy the rest of the night and escape the woman who wanted to spoil their fun.

Seconds later the compere stood up to make his announcement, and with the show running like clockwork, the curtain swung open to reveal the next act. The snake charmer, dressed in a pure white outfit with a bejewelled orange turban, drew gasps from the audience. They were terrified of Narendra and could not take their eyes off the serpent. The man sat in front of a small rattan basket, with a tin whistle, and mesmerised the lethal snake into submission. He and it swayed in unison until the end of the act, when the cobra sank back, and the man carefully replaced the lid.

After him, the little Hindi children performed a special dance with bells on their feet and ankles. They were dressed in loose clothing, fashioned from the brightest of colours. Each child had a small drum which they beat in a rhythm foreign to western ears.

Judging by the response of the crowd, one of the most popular acts was Maurice and his twelve little disciples. Judas, the instigator of much drama earlier, had star quality and stole the show. It was interesting to watch the transformation of Maurice's personality when he worked with his little followers. He trained them to pop out everywhere: from his sleeves, trouser legs and top hat. He made them disappear and reappear in strange places, but as he had said, they always came back to him. The magician ended his act with the twelve rabbits at his feet in a tight semi-circle. David was amazed by how the unruly little things could be organised when they wanted to be. He chuckled to himself. *Perhaps Maurice could work his magic on my unpredictable father?*

Granny Chong stood in the wings with an eagle eye on the twelve disciples, but Maurice was determined that the little bunnies would not end up in a chow mein. As soon as he left the stage, he marched the rabbits into their cages and locked each one shut, before asking a couple of the stagehands to whisk them back upstairs to safety in the attic's cubby hole.

The last act was to be the debut of the new diva, Simone Suileman. Max hoped she would have the gravitas to replace Monique and have the audience in the palm of her hand singing a few pub favourites and some festive tunes. David watched the delight on his father's face as a white-gloved hand appeared through the gap in the curtains and waved.

For some reason, the first few bars song made him feel sad. He looked at his watch, feeling more than ready to go home. *I hope she's less of a nuisance to deal with!* He swiftly corrected himself. *No one could be more of a nuisance than Monique.*

The hands pulled the curtain apart with a flourish. A young woman in an ordinary coat and floppy-brimmed hat appeared on stage as the music got louder. David was standing too far away from her to see her properly, and her hat kept her face in the shadows. She started to sing the famous song he had heard many times before.

> I'm a young girl and have just come over
> Over from the country where they do things
> big
> And amongst the boys I've got a lover
> And since I've got a lover—why I don't care a
> fig
>
> The boy I love is up in the gallery
> The boy I love is looking now at me
> There he is, can't you see, waving his
> handkerchief
> As merry as a robin that sings on a tree

Flashes of The Crown and Cushion came into his mind.

Could it be—?

Not taking his eyes off the woman, David ran up the steps that lead the stage. It was then he knew. He took off her hat and her dark hair tumbled down. As she finished the last line of her first song, he pulled her into his arms, not caring if the world was watching. He kissed her unashamedly.

"Here he is, the boy from the gallery!" Suzanna said when she had caught her breath.

Before she knew what was happening, David was kneeling before her.

"Get up, silly. What are you doing! You're ruining my opening night," she teased, trying tried to pull him up by the elbow. "Max, I need a bit of help here with this one!"

"I can see that," came the father's reply.

The audience laughed at the rapport between the young lovers. The moment was about to become more magical. David fumbled in his inside pocket.

"Suzanna Stratton, will you marry me?"

He flipped open the small box and revealed the glittering ring.

"Yes!" she shrieked in delight.

David slid the ring onto her delicate finger. It fitted perfectly. The audience cheered and whooped.

"Can you get back to the gallery and I get on with my set now?" she joked as she admired the sparkler on her finger.

The audience cheered again. That night, a new singer ruled the roost. Monique had faded into obscurity already. Instantly, Max put all the ideas of retirement to one side. *There is a new star to support.* As the night drew to a close, the crowd rushed out into the snow-covered street. Up above, the night sky sparkled with the crackle of fireworks.

The two lovebirds found themselves standing on a vast stage in an empty theatre. David had a puzzled expression. Things had moved so quickly.

"May I ask, Suzanna—what are you doing here? What happened to Florence?"

"I realised that if I chose a life of fame above a life with you, I would regret it for the rest of my life."

He took her in his arms and kissed her for a long time.

"As you are my favourite singer, can I take you to The Ritz for cocktails?"

"No, silly," laughed Suzanna. "Tonight, I just want us to be alone."

Printed in Great Britain
by Amazon